Unconditional

T0306434

Unconditional

Kelly Lawrence

LODESTONE
BOOKS

Winchester, UK
Washington, USA

First published by Lodestone Books, 2014
Lodestone Books is an imprint of John Hunt Publishing Ltd., Laurel House, Station Approach, Alresford, Hants, SO24 9JH, UK
office1@jhpbooks.net
www.johnhuntpublishing.com

For distributor details and how to order please visit the 'Ordering' section on our website.

Text copyright: Kelly Lawrence 2013

ISBN: 978 1 78279 394 6

All rights reserved. Except for brief quotations in critical articles or reviews, no part of this book may be reproduced in any manner without prior written permission from the publishers.

The rights of Kelly Lawrence as author have been asserted in accordance with the Copyright, Designs and Patents Act 1988.

A CIP catalogue record for this book is available from the British Library.

Design: Stuart Davies

Printed in the USA by Edwards Brothers Malloy

We operate a distinctive and ethical publishing philosophy in all areas of our business, from our global network of authors to production and worldwide distribution.

For Alannta, my own Princess, who is still at the age to appreciate a McDonalds. I love you sweetheart.

Chapter One

I love being in love. I love the wallowing and the dreamy sighing and the sheer wanting that goes with it all. In high school, I was in love with a boy called Roderick for four years. I gazed at him from across the classroom, scribbled our names together on my textbooks and on toilet walls, and listened to love songs over and over, convinced they were telling our story. Not that our relationship ever got past a few mumbled exchanges about homework. I got right through to sixth form without ever having a proper boyfriend, and only one kiss and a fumble, with Bradley Nicks from Chemistry, behind the sports hall. He tasted of ketchup and stolen cigarettes.

The first few months of college, I was in love with my history teacher. I tried to keep the gazing to a minimum, and thought myself a bit too sophisticated to be scribbling in my books like a schoolgirl, but I managed to construct a whole fantasy relationship in my head, with the help of my favourite pop ballads of course. When he left to be replaced by our current teacher Ms Ladgate, who smells of onions and has a squint, I was devastated. My best friend Dannii – she insists on the double vowel – shakes her head at me sadly.

'You need to get yourself a proper boyfriend, Ash. People are starting to think you're a secret lesbian.'

Truth is, I'm just not interested in the boys we hang around with; slouchy guys in hoodies or with boy band hair, whose main topics of conversation seem to be playing computer games online and which girl in which pop group they think is the hottest. I had liked Roderick because he was quiet and artistic, different from the usual crowd. Deep down, I'm pretty sure I'm different too. I mean, I have never been into smoking and trying to get into the latest clubs; what little popularity I have is mainly because of my friendship with Dannii. But it's not cool to be different, not unless you've got a group of friends that are different too, which doesn't make much sense. So I have to settle for being the nerdy friend of the popular crowd.

'I am not a secret lesbian.'

'I know, but people think you are. Even your mum thinks you are.'

'She does not!'

She probably does, if I'm honest. Mum has been asking me if I have a boyfriend 'yet' on a weekly basis since my fourteenth birthday, and her tone is becoming more and more desperate. I think she worries that I'm scarred from her break-up with my dad, who now lives in Australia with his new wife. She's also totally oblivious to the fact that all my male friends have major crushes on her, and only hang around the house to catch a glimpse of her. Mum was only sixteen when she had me, so she's not even thirty-five yet, and she's gorgeous, all copper curls and big blue eyes and petite curves. Dannii says I look like her, but I know I don't have her sparkle or charisma. Mum's an artist and scrapes a living illustrating children's books, just like Susan from Desperate Housewives, which used to be her favourite programme, except that we don't live in a fantastic house in the suburbs where everyone has perfect teeth. She's a bit quirky, but my mates think she's cool. Whereas I'm just a boring history buff. 'I don't want you to end up like me,' she's always saying. I should be so lucky.

'It doesn't matter if you are you know. Nobody cares these days.'

I look at Dannii nonplussed, totally confused.

'If you're a lesbian,' she says patiently. I start to protest again, then sigh as I see the corner of her mouth twist up in a smirk. She's just messing with me. Dannii after all knows about my penchant for impossible crushes and has long since given up trying to pair me off with any of our lad friends – most of whom are her cast offs anyway. Dannii goes through boyfriends like I go through books, and I'd probably be jealous of her if it wasn't the fact she's completely blasé about her own beauty. Unlike me, she's not a romantic at all.

Because it's not that I don't want a boyfriend; I just want it to be right. Unlike most of the girls we know I don't want a guy just because everyone else has one, and I've never been in a rush to get rid of my virginity. I want a guy who makes my heart race, who will make me feel special, not try to convince me a quick fumble round the back of McDonald's is a good idea.

'Right, I'm off. You're coming round later? Dean is coming, but he'll behave I promise.'

I roll my eyes but nod and agree to walk round later when I've wrestled with my latest essay. Dean is her latest guy. He's two years older than us but acts about twelve, in my opinion, but he seems harmless enough and is typically smitten with Dannii.

As I'm walking up the path to my house I can hear Mum singing away to herself, which means she's painting and in a good mood. I pop my head in the front room cum studio and she waves at me. There's a big blob of red acrylic on her cheek and she has that fevered look she gets when she's in the middle of a project.

'How was school?'

'College, Mum.' I wish I'd gone to a further away college sometimes instead of staying on round here; it seems so much more grown up, even if I would have been doing the same subjects. I want to go on to study history at university, and although I always tell my teachers I want to be a research historian, what I really want to do, if I'm honest, is write trashy historical romances. Dannii is the only person who knows that. She's at college with me only because she didn't want to move away without me; mainly because I always do her homework. Her secret ambition is to be a footballer's wife.

I turn my attention back to Mum, who rolls her eyes.

'Well, how was your day then?'

'Same as always,' I shrug. Mum nods and goes back to her canvas, waving a hand at her empty cup on the side. I pick it up and go into the kitchen to make her coffee. She drinks it like it's going out of fashion when she's painting.

'Your dad phoned,' she calls after me. 'I told him you'd ring him when you got in'.

That's unusual. Dad has phoned three times this week already. Since he got married to Anya I'm lucky if he phones three times a month. I'm supposed to be going over for the summer holidays, but can't help feeling a bit disloyal to Mum. They split when I was twelve, but it's only been the past eighteen months or so that she's been smiling again.

'I'll ring him later,' I mutter, even though she can't hear me. As I put the kettle on, Sabre, our German Shepherd, comes over and nudges my leg with his head, looking at me with that dopey look dogs give you and I let him out into the garden, laughing as he attempts to pounce on a bird and head butts the lawn. For a breed of dog reported to be intelligent Sabre is about as dumb as you can get. Dad bought him for my eleventh birthday.

Thinking of Dad, I sigh and pick up the phone in the hall. May as well get it over and done with, I tell myself.

'Hey, Princess,' he says, his usual greeting that always makes me wince, though he never notices. 'How was school?'

'It's college,' I say wearily, 'and it's fine thanks.'

He goes quiet, and for the first time I realise there might be a reason why he's called me so much this week.

'Do you fancy doing something this weekend?'

'You're not in Australia?'

'I'm staying at Granma's for a while. Me and Anya are, ah, having a few problems.'

My heart starts to race for reasons I'm not sure of.

'You've broke up? Does Mum know?'

But of course she would. Granma hates Anya and would have told her straight away. I wonder if that's why she's been extra perky this week. I hope not. It's taken us long enough to get used to the way things are.

'I believe so. So, about the weekend?'

I shrug, then realise that of course he can't see me.

'Yeah, sure.'

'Okay, Princess, I'll pick you up Saturday.'

He's still saying goodbye as I put the phone down and go in to Mum.

'Dad and Anya have split up.'

Mum just nods absentmindedly, frowning at the canvas in front of her.

'Did you make the coffee?' She looks up, sees my face and sighs.

'I thought he should tell you. It's not really my business, honey. Are you okay?'

I nod, surprised at her total nonchalance. Does she really not care? Still, four years is a long time, and Mum's dated since. She went out with a guy called Barry for nearly a year, until she came back from work and caught him smoking weed in front of me. I've still never told her about the time he actually offered me some, she'd have a fit.

'What are you working on?' I nod towards the canvas.

Mum looks excited, and Dad and his love life – or lack of it – are forgotten as she gushes on about a new commission she's working on designing covers for a new series of 'Spy Boy' books. She's passionate about her work and really gets engrossed in it, but even so, I thought she would have some opinion on the subject. They were married for like, forever.

'What are you doing tonight?' she asks.

'I'm going round Dannii's,' I tell her. 'To study.'

'Study what? You don't even take the same subjects.' Mum laughs. 'Just don't be drinking or smoking, okay? Is her boyfriend going round? Brian, isn't it? Maybe he'll have some nice friends.'

Here we go. 'It's Dean now,' I mumble, backing out of the room, 'and I don't think he's got any friends.' I go up to my room before she can start quizzing me and pull out my history books, ready to lose myself in the Age of Enlightenment for an hour or so.

Half an hour later I'm not feeling very enlightened, having just been staring at the page wondering what's going on with my dad, and what the knock on effects will be. I feel guilty for not being happier that he's back in the country, but can't help having a sense of foreboding about the whole thing. It's way too early to go to Dannii's so I pick up the latest romance I'm reading, but can't get into that either. I fuss around tidying my room, go and make myself and Mum a sandwich – she forgets to feed herself when she's painting – and then remember the new skinny jeans I brought last week and try them on. In spite of the fact that I've always thought my butt was too big for skinnies, I have to admit they look pretty good. Dannii picked them; she's got a real eye for things that will suit people, and according to her, big booties are in. I'm sure she's trying to make me feel better about my B cup boobs, her having been a D since we were fifteen, but there's no denying the jeans make me look cute. I find myself wishing Mr Bryant the lush history teacher was still around to see them, then decide my mum and Dannii might be right; maybe I do need a proper boyfriend. Before I'm doomed to spend my life living with Mum, who probably has more of a love life than I do, sitting in my room reading crappy romance novels and growing cobwebs.

I wear my skinny jeans with a tight red tee that makes me actually look like I've got some breasts and scrunch up my curls. With my leather jacket and new boots, I look pretty cool. Not like a history buff at all. Mum stares at me on my way out of the door, then just smiles and nods.

'Don't be late, honey, and phone me if you need anything,' she chirps. I'm never late; sometimes I think she wishes I would do something rebellious. Nothing crazy like setting fire to the school, just coming home a bit drunk with my hair dyed pink or something. After all at my age she was married with a baby.

I walk to Dannii's pretty slowly, still thinking about Dad and Anya. When I get there her mother's already out and she ushers me in with a wide smile. Her eyes look slightly glazed, which means she's been drinking already, and no doubt Dean is already here.

'Do you want a drink?'

'Coke is fine.' She ignores me and thrusts a beer into my hand and I follow her through to her room. She's got the best room, it's practically her own little apartment with her own bathroom and everything. Dean is lounging on the bed, rolling what I doubt is just tobacco, and there's another guy on the sofa in front of Dannii's plasma. I'd love my own plasma.

'Hey, babe,' Dean says in his usual drawl, not looking up from what he's doing. I perch on the edge of the bed, not wanting to go and sit next to the other boy, who hasn't even turned round to acknowledge me.

'Hi. How was work?' Dean works at the local pool hall, which is where Dannii met him, after noticing him staring down her top every time she bent over the table. That's still pretty much his favourite past time. As I pull off my jacket I notice him look at my own outfit, lingering on my boosted cleavage. He wolf whistles, and Dannii elbows him in annoyance, but I can tell by her face she's not really that bothered. I can't work out what she sees in Dean at all. He's good-looking, I guess, and all over her when he's not stoned, but any trace of a personality has been hidden deep.

'You do look great, babe,' she tells me, winking. 'I told you to get those jeans didn't I?' She high-fives me and I laugh, blushing. If I'm honest, the compliments are nice. I'm so used to fading into the background next to Dannii; being the clever one while she's the pretty one, that they don't tend to come my way very often.

'See, Joe, I told you she was a hottie,' Dean says to the boy on the sofa, who turns around to look at us with a bored expression on his face. His eyes sweep over me and I think I see a flicker of approval, but then his face shuts down and goes blank.

'Yeah,' he nods, as if he doesn't think so at all, and turns back to the TV, taking a swig of his beer. I flush, in embarrassment this time. How rude, I mouth silently to Dannii, who shrugs.

'That's Joe, Dean's friend. Joe, this is my best girl friend, Ashley.' She says it in a mock formal tone, and the boy turns around again, regarding me with that blank expression. His eyes, though unreadable, are strangely intense. As I look at him fully, I feel a tightening in my belly as I realise just how gorgeous he is. He has dark blonde hair cut close to his head, not in one of the stupid floppy styles most boys seem to favour, and almost amber coloured eyes with lashes Dannii would have to stick on to achieve. A full lush mouth too, which is my favourite part on a boy. I gulp. From what I can see of him over the sofa, his arms in his white tee are tanned and muscular. He hasn't got that gangly look most guys in their late teens seem to have. He must work out. A lot.

'Hi,' he says at last, almost amused as if he's caught me checking him out. I smile shyly and go to say 'hi' back, but he's already turned around again. I put my head down feeling almost rejected. Dannii sticks her tongue out at the back of his head.

'Ignore him, he's always moody,' she says, and I wonder how many times she's met him. I've never heard her mention him, though to be fair I tend to zone out any time she starts talking about anything to do with Dean.

Dean blows a heavy cloud of smoke into the air and the unmistakable smell of weed fills the room. I turn my face away, not wanting it to make me cough, especially in front of Joe, which is stupid, because he's not even looking at me. I feel uncomfortable now and wish I hadn't bothered coming round, but I can't leave so quickly without offending Dannii and besides, what else would I do?

'My dad phoned today,' I tell Dannii. 'He's split up with Anya. I'm going to see him at the weekend.'

'Your dad's hot,' Dannii says and I sigh. There's no point in talking to her about it now, not when she's had a beer. She takes a drag of Dean's joint and then offers it to me, grinning. She always does this, even though she knows I'll say no. The one time I tried it I had a coughing fit and then felt sick for an hour. I shake my head at her and shoot her an annoyed look, which she pretends not to see, then takes another drag before passing it back to Dean. She lies back on the bed and entwines her arm through mine, squeezing my bicep.

'You okay?' she murmurs and I nod, unable to stay annoyed at her. We can always read each other's moods, we've been friends for so long.

'You want some of this, Joe?' Dean asks his friend, who looks over and shakes his head with a touch of contempt.

'Nah, man.'

For some reason, I feel pleased that he didn't accept it.

'Go fetch some more beer then,' Dean says. .Joe sighs and gets up, going into the kitchen. I look at Dannii.

'What's his problem?'

'He's got to stay out of trouble,' Dean answers for her, assuming I'm referring to Joe saying no to the weed rather than his rudeness. 'He's on probation, he's not long out of juvy.'

Young offenders jail? I had assumed he was about nineteen, same as Dean, but he must be mine and Dannii's age then. He looks older than seventeen, especially with that build. As he had walked past into the kitchen I couldn't help noticing his arms matched the rest of him; he's built like an action movie star. Probably from working out in jail, I realise. I don't suppose there's much else to do.

'What did he do wrong?'

'Dunno.' Dannii answers me this time. 'Fighting, I think.'

She goes to say something else then stops as Joe comes back in and tosses a four pack of beer on the bed after removing one for himself.

'Ash is okay, it'll take her an hour to drink that one,' Dannii quips, and Joe looks at me. Those intense amber coloured eyes linger on my body, then my face, but dart away as soon as he catches my eye. I can't work out if he approves of what he sees or not, and as he stalks back off to resume his seat on the sofa I tell myself I don't care. He's clearly bad news.

'Joe lives on the Estate,' Dannii says, referring to the roughest part of town, 'near Rianne.' Rianne is our friend, who dropped out of school last year after getting pregnant. She was closer to Dannii than me, but ever since she left school I've seen more of her.

'I might go see her at the weekend,' I tell Dannii. 'Why don't you come? She always asks after you.'

Dannii pulls a face. 'Urgh, babies,' is all she says. I sometimes get the impression Dannii looks down on her for being silly enough to get pregnant and then as if that wasn't dumb enough, actually keeping it.

Joe has turned to face us again and is glaring at Dannii. At first I think it's her comment about Rianne's baby, until he snaps at her.

'I live with my aunt. She's a good woman,' he says, as if angry that Dannii has revealed where he lives and wants to make it sound better. He shoots me a look I can't fathom before getting up and pulling his jacket on.

'You going, mate?' Dean asks, surprised. Joe nods.

'Yeah, I'm pretty tired. See you all later,' he throws over his shoulder, and is gone without even looking at me. I feel irritated and deflated at the same time.

'Well, he's talkative,' I say sarcastically to no one in particular. Dannii looks at me slyly.

'Do you like him?'

'Not at all. I've never met a guy so rude; he must really think he's something,' I snap at her, but she rolls her eyes and I know she's not convinced. The truth is, Joe has affected me somehow; I want to see him again and yet at the same time can't think of anything worse. Although I doubt he would be interested as he clearly wasn't impressed, skinny jeans or not. He's probably into girls that wear skin-tight clothes, have piercings and swear a lot.

And are most definitely not virgins.

'He's not that bad,' Dean chimes in. 'He's just had a rough time, and he's actually a pretty good guy. Big heart, you know?'

Me and Dannii look at Dean in complete shock that he's actually tried to say something intelligent, and he goes red and resumes puffing on his joint.

'Bless, I think they might have a bit of a 'bromance' on the go,' Dannii quips and I laugh, but I'm thinking over Dean's comment and wondering what Joe's story is. I can't help it; there's something intriguing about him, something that has grabbed my attention even more than the unfathomable amber eyes and the mouth that was just made for kissing. I bet he would be a good kisser. Better than Bradley, at any rate.

The next hour or so drags completely, and I end up on the sofa by myself watching music videos while Dannii and Dean giggle and probably grope each other on the bed. I let enough time pass that it doesn't look like I'm being rude, and then announce I'm tired. Dannii insists they walk me home.

'It's dark out there, babe, your mum will go mad.'

So we walk back, the three of us, with Dannii in the middle holding both our arms and giggling from too much beer, while Dean slopes along with a serene, stoned smile.

'What are you two up to now?' I ask, wondering if I should invite them in. Dannii snuggles up closer to her boyfriend.

'He's staying at mine. Aren't you, babe?' she says and Dean grins lasciviously. I hope she's not sleeping with him already, but now is hardly the time to ask. It amazes me that her mum never seems to care. For as much as I know my mother worries I'm not rebelling as much as I should, I'm pretty sure she wouldn't let me have a boy stay over that I had only known a few months. One thing she has drummed into me is not to get pregnant as young as she did. Almost as if she regrets having me, though I'd never say that to her.

We reach the outside of my house and Mum appears on the porch as I'm hugging Dannii goodbye.

'Hi, love. Hello, Dannii, and Dylan, is it?'

'It's Dean,' Dannii corrects her, while Dean stands there staring at Mum with his tongue hanging out. I usher her in while Dannii elbows him again, looking genuinely pissed off this time.

'Bye, guys,' I call as she drags him back off down the street.

Mum looks tired, no doubt from painting all day, but before I can ask her if she's okay she kisses me on the forehead and announces she's off to bed. I go up myself, hanging black jeans and a sweater on the door for school tomorrow and then falling into bed. I pick up my novel, then discard it.

My last thought before I drift off to sleep is that there must surely be more to life than this, and the last face I see in my mind before all goes blank is Joe's, curling his mouth and raising an eyebrow at me almost as if in challenge.

Chapter Two

'You look great,' Dad enthuses, and I smile. I have my skinnies on again and my leather jacket, though with a less revealing top. I'm about to say thank you when I realise he isn't looking at me at all, but straight past me at Mum who if there was any justice shouldn't look great as she's covered in paint and her hair's all crazy, but the look suits her. Me, I'd just look a mess.

'You don't,' Mum says to him, but she's smiling. They stand in the hall giving each other goofy grins until I clear my throat loudly. This is not good.

Dad turns to me as if he's only just remembered I'm the reason he's actually here.

'You ready, Princess? I thought we could go for a McDonalds?'

He really does still think I'm about twelve.

'Sure. Bye, Mum.' She kisses me on the cheek, but her eyes are on Dad.

As I get in the car, I notice in the sunlight that Dad looks older. Okay, I've not seen him for months but he looks years older; his face more lined and drawn and he's lost weight. He's only thirty-seven, but he looks older than that now, I think. He notices me looking at him and smiles sadly.

'Belt up. Sorry it's been a while since I've been over, but things will be different now.'

I bite back a retort, but can't help thinking that it shouldn't take him splitting up with Anya for him to bother making an effort.

'What happened?' I ask. No point beating around the bush. Dad drives off and doesn't answer until we've turned onto the main road.

'I think she's met someone else.' He says it in a matter of

fact way, like it's all fine, but I know it's not. He must be devastated. I always thought if something like this happened I would say he deserves it for leaving Mum, but now I just feel desperately sad for him.

'I'm sorry.'

He just nods and pats my knee. It's not enough, but I don't know what else to say. Asking too many questions would just be insensitive, and anyway, what do I know about relationships?

We get to McDonalds and on a whim I order the nuggets, fries and doughnut I always had as a kid. It's nice to just be here with Dad again. I find a booth in the corner and settle in while Dad comes over with the food. I'm really looking forward to my nuggets.

'Have you thought about which university you want to go to?' Dad asks. I nod and start to tell him I'm thinking Birmingham, but then realise he's looking out of the window and not really listening. His face has gone all tight, and I bet he's thinking about Anya. His next question though is definitely not about Anya.

'How's Keira? Your mum I mean. She looks as fantastic as ever, and I hear the design work is going well?'

I laugh. 'You know Mum, she's always got a million projects on at once, but yeah, I think things are pretty good for her.' I don't bother mentioning that we're finally back on our feet after he left and forced Mum to sell the house.

'Good, I'm really pleased for her.' He looks it too, in fact it's the most animated I've seen him since he picked me up, and again I can't help thinking that this isn't good. He seems more interested in her than me.

'So you'll be sticking around for a while then?'

'Possibly. I have a meeting on Monday about a vacancy that may be coming up not too far away.'

Like Mum, he's a designer, but of really boring stuff like

car parts and machines. Guy stuff. I know that's sexist, but still.

'It will be nice to be able to see more of you, Ash. I've missed so much of your life these past few years.'

'You didn't have to,' I point out then feel immediately awful as he just looks devastated. I concentrate on my doughnut. 'This is really good,' I tell him even though it tastes like cardboard. I'm trying to think of something cheery to say but then Dad speaks first.

'Any boys on the horizon?' His tone is jokey but his eyes, over the rim of his coffee, are serious.

I shake my head, even as Joe's face pops into my mind. I don't know why I've thought of him, he barely said two words to me the other night and couldn't have been less interested. A couple of intense looks, but they could have meant anything. Maybe he just didn't like my hair.

He's hardly the type of boy I would usually go for anyway, he's got trouble written all over him. He's gorgeous, but that's as far as it goes. He probably knows it too, and has girls after him left, right and centre. Definitely more Dannii's type than mine, though he would probably be too high maintenance for her if that surly attitude is typical of him.

I can't deny it though, as much as I may want to, he's been on my mind a lot the last few days since I first saw him. I caught myself daydreaming about kissing that gorgeous mouth in a class I'm usually really interested in and had to stop myself quizzing Dannii for more information about him. Perhaps it's the challenge, the whole unobtainable thing, like with my previous crushes. Yet it feels different. I don't want to think about him, I'm actively trying not to, and he certainly doesn't seem like someone I would even get on with, and yet whenever I do, I get a little rush in my belly that I never felt when I was swooning over

Roderick or a handsome teacher.

'Are you sure?' Dad's peering at me and I realise I'm blushing. Again. I hate being pale.

'No one special,' I say, and he just looks worried. Great, now he probably thinks I sleep around.

We make small talk for a bit then we drive to Granma's, who fusses over me and gives me cake. It's late afternoon before I remember I was going to visit Rianne today. When I ask Dad to drive me there instead of home I'm sure he looks disappointed. Does he really think he could have another chance with Mum?

Apparently so, as it's the first thing he says when we get back into the car.

'So, your mum hasn't met anyone yet then?' He tries to sound nonchalant, but the look of relief when I shake my head is pitifully obvious.

'I'm surprised, she's a beautiful woman. You look exactly like her at that age you know.'

It always makes me feel funny to think that when Mum was my age, they had already had me. Although we're close she's always drummed it into me how hard it was having a baby so young, and I can't help thinking that's maybe another reason I've held off on the whole boyfriend thing. Rianne always looks so tired and stressed out now, having Gabriel seems to have aged her about ten years. And she swears blind she was on the Pill.

Dad looks concerned when he drops me off at her house; a little two up two down right in the middle of the roughest street on the Estate.

'Do you want me to pick you up later?'

'I'll be fine,' I reassure him. 'I'll call Mum if it's late.'

He tuts and gives me the money for a cab, before letting me out and driving off with a little wave over his shoulder. I wave back, feeling bad for my mean comment earlier. I suppose it would be kind of nice if he did stick around.

Rianne opens the door looking wild-eyed and I can hear little Gabriel squawking away in the background.

'He's been like this for *hours,*' she moans, ushering me in. She's lost weight, and there are bags under her eyes that you could carry your shopping in.

In the poky front room Gabriel lies screaming in one of those swingy chair things. Rianne picks him up, putting him over her shoulder and patting his back. He stops for a second and looks up at her, then promptly starts screaming again, his little face all scrunched up and red. Rianne looks up at the clock.

'He's due a bottle now so he might sleep after, thank God. Here, just hold him a minute.' She passes the baby to me and hurries into the kitchen.

I freeze, holding a screaming Gabriel in my lap as if he's made of china. I've held him a few times and even changed him once but he's never been crying like this before, and the way he's writhing around I'm terrified I'm going to drop him. He looks up at me accusingly with his bright blue eyes full of tears, and I feel an almost primal urge to comfort him, though I wouldn't have a clue where to start.

Rianne comes back and he reaches for her as soon as he sees the bottle in her hands. As soon as he's on her lap being fed, his tears disappear and he closes his eyes, making cute sucking noises on the bottle.

'Where's Mitch?' I ask, referring to her boyfriend and Gabriel's dad.

'At his mums, getting some sleep. He's on nights at the factory, and with Gabe screaming like this all day he needs some peace.'

Mitch is a good guy, he's stood by her and works long hours to provide for them all, but it means she's on her own a lot, and they're both exhausted. He's only eighteen; he was going to college to study engineering until Rianne fell pregnant. I can't help wondering if they ever regret their decision, but I'd never ask her that. It must have been like this for Mum and Dad once.

'How's Dannii? Is she still with that Brian?'

Shows how close her and Dannii are now.

'She's started seeing that Dean Smith, the one that works at Rileys.'

Rianne pulls a face and I laugh. Clearly she thinks as much of Dean's credentials as a boyfriend as I do. Before I can stop myself, I ask her, 'Do you know his friend Joe? He lives round here somewhere apparently. I met him at hers the other day, but he was like, really rude.'

Rianne's eyes light up.

'The new guy who's moved in to Mr Roger's old house with his mum? Yeah, he's like seriously hot.'

'That's the one. It's his aunt, he said.' I wonder again what his story is. Maybe his parents disowned him after his stint in jail.

Rianne raises her eyebrows at me knowingly.

'You like him.' It's a statement, not a question. I squirm in my seat, feeling uncomfortable.

'I only met him the once. I think he's got an attitude problem.' I sound snappy, and wonder why I'm being so defensive. Rianne just smiles.

'You do like him,' she says again, a bit triumphantly. I ignore her and coo at Gabriel, who's looking at me over his bottle. He gives me a look of disdain and closes his eyes, gripping his bottle as if he thinks someone might take it. He's so adorable, at least now he's stopped crying.

'He's bad news,' I say. 'Dean said he's just got out of juvy.'

'I didn't know that. Still' —Rianne looks thoughtful— 'you don't know what he's done. You shouldn't judge a book by its cover and all that. You want to see some of the looks I got when I was walking around here with a big belly on me. As if I'm some skank and don't know who the dad is.'

I suppose she's got a point. Whether it's teen pregnancy or delinquency, people are always too quick to point the finger.

'My mum and dad got married; maybe that's what you and Mitch should do,' I suggest, and Rianne squeals with laughter.

'Babe! It is the twenty-first century you know! Besides' —she looks thoughtful again— 'we couldn't afford it.'

She goes quiet, and I'm grateful that all I have to worry about financially is saving up enough tips from the café I work at twice a week to afford new jeans. Rianne sits the baby up to pat his back, and as soon as she touches him he lets out a massive burp then hiccups up some milk, making us both laugh. He's asleep within minutes, and Rianne lets out a sigh of relief. She looks so exhausted I think I should head off and let her get some sleep, but when I suggest it she looks at me in horror.

'I need some company,' she pleads, 'and conversation other than babies.' Though after twenty minutes of talking music and boys we're talking about Gabe again, his sleeping patterns – or lack of them – and the teething remedies she's tried. I don't even think she realises she's doing it, so I nod and smile and try to look like I've got a clue what she's talking about. Gabriel wakes up after an hour or so and Rianne starts running a bath, so I say my goodbyes feeling guilty that I'm glad to go. I wish there was more I could do to help, but it's all so alien to me. Maybe I could ask Mum to babysit and get Rianne out for a bit; though by the look of her she'd probably prefer a few hours sleep.

Walking home I'm glad I've left before dark; usually walking through the Estate doesn't bother me but for some reason this evening it feels creepy, looking grimy and foreboding in the evening half-light. It used to be nice round here, Dad always said, but now every few houses there's a broken down car or a boarded-up window. I should have got a cab, and I pull out my phone to call one but realise my battery has gone flat. I dither for a minute, wondering whether to go back to Rianne's and ring one but not wanting to disturb her in the middle of putting the baby to bed. Instead I decide to take the short cut through the park, reasoning that it's no less dangerous than walking through the whole Estate and at least it's quicker; the other side of the park is only twenty minutes from my house. I really need to learn to drive; Mum's got some money put away for my first car but says I have to put in towards the lessons. I keep meaning to, but there's always a new book or clothes that I want.

As soon as I'm into the park properly and walking past the play area I realise my mistake. A group of guys are draped over the swings and climbing frames, smoking and drinking and talking in low voices. They all look up as they see me coming and the one nearest to me smirks. I wish I had the dog with me. I shove my hands in my pockets and walk with my head down, hoping they won't bother me and cursing myself for deciding to walk home.

'Hey, Ash,' one of them calls, and I look up, recognising one of the boys from school a couple of years ago. I think he dropped out before exams. His name's Adam something or other, and he's one of those slouchy guys who always look a bit menacing and look at you like they're imagining you with your clothes off. I smile and wave, picking my pace up, but he comes jogging after me with his mates behind him. He comes to a halt in front of me, forcing me to stop. I go to walk on the grass to go around him but he steps with me so he's still in my way. I roll my eyes, trying to pretend he's just being a pain, but my heart is hammering and his friends have caught up and are clustering round.

'Where are you off to then?' he asks.

'Just on my way home.'

'Already? It's a Saturday night, why don't you come and have a drink with us?'

I shake my head.

'Nah, I've got stuff to do at home. Thanks though.' I smile as if I'm really pleased at his kind offer and go to step forward again, but he crosses his arms and doesn't budge. A lock of greasy hair falls over his forehead from under his cap and he pushes it away in irritation. I notice how dirty his fingernails are. Behind me, his friends are sniggering.

'We're going to a club later. Come with us.' He really doesn't like taking no for an answer.

I glare at him and say as firmly as I can. 'Like I said, I've got stuff to do. Would you mind getting out of my way?'

Adam just laughs, and not in a nice way. One of the other guys nudges me from behind so that I almost fall into Adam and I spin round glaring, much to his friend's amusement. There are two boys hanging back a bit, the one who pushed me who is small and ferrety looking and a taller, stockier lad who isn't laughing but looking at me with a sneer. I'm betting he's the ringleader, and the reason Adam is showing off.

'Maybe I would mind,' Adam says from behind me, so close I can feel his breath on the back of my neck. I tense, wishing I had kept up those self-defence classes last year and trying to remember everything I learnt at the two I went to, when I was actually paying attention and not laughing at Dannii trying to flirt with the instructor. No doubt if Dannii was here she'd flirt her way out of it.

The taller guy speaks, looking me up and down with undisguised contempt.

'She doesn't want to drink with us. Thinks she's too good for us don't you?'

I shake my head in protest. 'I'm just busy,' I begin, but I hear Adam's voice again, not even pretending to be friendly now.

'Yeah, I bet she does. You were always stuck up at school weren't you, Ash? Little Miss Goody-two-shoes. Not like that mate of yours.'

'Who's her mate?' the ferret-faced one asks, leering at me.

'Dannii something. Let me feel her tits for a few smokes. Jason's had a go on her too.'

The taller one, who must be Jason, finally cracks a smile, though it's more of a smirk. He takes a long swig from his bottle of Bud and gives me a long look.

'Yeah.' He nods. 'She's a right slut.'

'She is not!' I snap. I've never heard her mention a Jason; they're just trying to wind me up. It's had the desired effect, as Jason laughs and goes 'oooh' sarcastically.

'Why are you hanging around with her then?' Ferret Boy pipes up. 'If she's a slut and you're stuck up? She can't be that stuck up, Ads, I bet she's a little goer really.'

I've had enough of this. I turn to face Adam, trying not to cringe away, as he's so close I can smell his fag and beer breath.

'I really need to go, Adam. Maybe we can catch up another time?'

But my pretty pathetic attempt at appeasing him falls flat. Instead he pulls me towards him. I push at his chest, but he just laughs, and his mates are crowding up behind me.

'How about we catch up right now?' he leans right in as if he's going to kiss me. Okay, now I'm seriously scared.

'Let me go!' I shout and try to twist away but one of the others pushes me again from behind, harder this time, so I have to clutch at Adam to steady myself.

'Told you she's up for it,' the one called Jason crows and grabs me from behind. I thrust an elbow into his stomach, and he winces but doesn't let go.

'Little bitch.' Now I've just pissed them off. I open my mouth to scream, then hear another boy's voice shouting over the park.

'Hey!' We all turn towards him but they don't let go of me.

'What's going on?' The voice sounds familiar and as he comes up to us I realise it's none other than Dean's friend Joe. My heart sinks at the thought he might be involved with Adam and his crowd.

'Ash?' he recognises me and looks from Adam to Jason and back again. 'What's going on?' he asks again.

'We're just having a laugh,' Adam says, defensive. He lets go of me. Jason doesn't, in fact he tightens his grip on my waist even as I try to wrench away.

'She doesn't look like she's having a lot of fun. Ash?'

'They won't let me go,' I admit. Joe steps towards us and everyone apart from Jason steps away from me.

'Let her go,' he says, and although he hasn't raised his voice and his face hasn't changed there's a weird undertone that is very, very menacing. Adam starts gabbling. 'We were just messing around, mate,' he says, raising his hands. Jason lets go too, but takes a step towards Joe. Oh God, they're going to fight.

'What's it to you?'

Joe doesn't answer, instead staring at Jason long and hard until the taller boy drops his eyes. Whatever their weird silent exchange was, Joe clearly won.

'Sorry, mate, I didn't realise she was with you,' Jason mumbles, though he doesn't sound sorry at all. They slope off, Adam giving me an apologetic smile. I flip my finger at him, feeling brave now.

'Thanks,' I say to Joe gratefully, but he just glares at me.

'What were you doing hanging around with those idiots?'

He sounds really angry.

'I wasn't,' I snap back, folding my arms around myself feeling suddenly cold. 'I was on my way home.'

'On your own? Around here? Are you stupid?' He looks furious now, and I'm not sure if I'm any safer with him than I was with Adam and his cronies. I mean, he just frightened all five of them off just by looking at them. I feel a bit like the heroine from one of my romance novels, thought the hero is usually a dashing English lord, not a moody teenage boy with a criminal record.

'Well, anyway, thanks,' I say again and go to walk off. He follows me.

'I'm walking you home,' he says when I look at him in surprise, 'to make sure you don't get yourself into any more trouble. They're bad guys, Ash, you don't want to be mixing with them.'

'How do you know them then?'

'Just from round here. That Jason tried to make friends when we moved in, until I made it clear I think he's a jerk. Now he wants to fight me.'

I think about that.

'Why didn't he fight you then?' After all, I think, he had his friends to back him up. Joe laughs, but there's no mirth in it.

'Because he'd lose. He won't risk being shown up in front of his little friends.'

He seems so sure of himself.

'Why did you help me?' I ask, and he looks at me and shakes his head in disgust.

'Why wouldn't I? You think I'm like them?'

I shake my head but he just tuts and looks away. We walk on in silence. As we get out of the other end of the park I want to tell him I'm all right from here, but he carries on walking and I don't say anything. If I'm honest, I'm starting to feel a bit shaky as I wonder what would have happened if he hadn't turned up. I sneak a look at him. He's got a great profile, and he walks very straight, like a soldier, not all slouchy and lazy like Dean or Adam.

'How old are you?' I blurt out, wondering if I've got things wrong. If I hadn't met him with Dean, I might have thought he was about twenty-one.

'I turned eighteen last week,' he said, without looking at me.

'Do you drive?'

He looks irritated by my questions.

'I can, but I don't have a car,' he says shortly. Perhaps he just got into trouble for driving offences then. We lapse back into silence. He's really not much of a talker, this guy.

Then he surprises me by asking, a few streets later, 'Dannii told me you liked to read?'

'I'm a bit of a geek,' I admit.

'Not at all. I like to read. Got into it when I was locked up, there's not much else to do. Apart from the gym.'

Well he obviously spent a lot of time there, judging by his physique. I'm staring again and he notices, this time giving me a little half-smile that's almost shy. I feel ridiculously pleased.

'What did you do?' I blurt out.

'Got into a fight with a boy at my school. He was a bully; I caught him picking on some little lad.'

Playing the hero again. But I'm not silly, I know enough to know you don't get sent to juvy for scaring off bullies. I say so, and he looks at me and sort of laughs.

'Nosey aren't you? But you're right. I lost my temper, lost control, really laid into him and in front of people too. When it went to court, the boy I'd been defending in the first place was too scared of the bullies to give a statement in my defence. So now everyone thinks I'm just a thug.'

He sounds bleak. I touch his arm, wanting to comfort him. I'm not usually this bold around a guy, but hey, he did just rescue me.

'I don't think you're a thug. Well, not now anyway. You didn't hurt Jason or Adam.'

He grins at me. It's the first time I've seen him properly smile and he looks younger and more boyish. My tummy does this weird little flip.

'What do you mean, 'not now?' You're funny.'

He really seems to find me amusing. Well, at least he's not glaring at me anymore.

'Well, at Dannii's you were kind of rude, and she said you'd been in jail for fighting. So it wasn't the best first impression.'

His smile vanishes. I've offended him again.

'Sorry.'

'Huh?' I wasn't expecting that.

'For being rude.'

I don't know what to say to that, so we walk on again in silence, but it's a more comfortable one now. I'm thinking over everything he's said when something occurs to me.

'Why did Dannii tell you I like reading? We hadn't even met.'

He looks embarrassed.

'Dean was trying to set us up. I told him I wasn't interested.'

I can't stop my face falling, and he continues in a rush.

'In girls in general I mean. That was before I saw you.'

So what does that mean, that he is interested? My stomach's in knots I realise I want him to be, very badly. I wait for him to say something else but he's gone quiet again and we're not far from my street now.

'So, are you going round Dannii's this week?' As if that doesn't make it obvious I want to see him again.

'Maybe. I'm at work all this week, at the garage near Dean's.'

'You're a mechanic?' I can't help imagining him in overalls, all oily. My mum has one of those old Athena posters from when she was younger, the one that features the guy with his top off, carrying tyres and looking stupidly hot. I can just see Joe in the same pose, and the thought makes my face hot, and not just with embarrassment.

'I'm great with cars,' he says proudly. 'I want my own garage when I'm older.'

'You're lucky to get a job so quick, I mean with having a record.' That was insensitive, I'm such a dork sometimes. But he doesn't seem to mind, he just nods, agreeing with me.

'Yeah, I know. My boss, Bob, knows all about it and still gave me a chance. There are some good people around.' He shoots a sideways glance at me as if he thinks I'm one of those good people, or maybe he means he is, in spite of his recent past. I think about my statement to Rianne earlier that he was bad news and feel mean, but I don't know him well enough to know that the version of events he's given me is true do I? Though instinct tells me he's being straight with me.

I'm trying to think of a way to make it clear I want to see him again without making it too obvious. I couldn't even give him my number if he asked for it, because my phone's dead and I don't know my own number off by heart. There's no way I'm asking for his, that's way too forward.

'This is my road,' I say as we turn into my street.

'It's nice,' he says shortly. It's just a typical street, I think, but I suppose compared to the Estate it must seem a lot different. It seems to bother him, where he lives, and it occurs to me that he thinks I'll look down on him. We reach my house and I stop, desperately searching for something to say. I almost want to invite him in, but I don't want Mum grilling him and making him retreat into his shell again. But if I just go in I'll kick myself for not saying something.

'Are you on Facebook?' I ask, cringing as I hear myself say it. Dannii's obsessed with it and I'm always teasing her about it, now it seems like a great way to communicate.

'We don't have the internet.'

Of course not. Now he looks cross again, and I feel stupid. I shift from one foot to the other.

'Well, maybe I'll see you around then. Thanks for earlier.' I turn to walk up my path but he touches my hand. I look at him, surprised.

'Ash, promise me you won't go walking round there at night on your own again?' His voice is soft.

'I promise,' I say, touched by his concern. He smiles, a real smile again that lights his whole face up, transforming him from a slightly intimidating – but very sexy – guy to a happy teenager. It's like the sun suddenly coming out on a miserable day.

God, I've got it bad. Then I realise he's looking at my mouth. Hardly daring to hope, I step towards him slightly, fizzing with nerves.

And he does it, he kisses me. Leans down and brushes my lips with his in a way that makes me tingle all over. I wrap my arms round him and kiss him back hungrily, all shyness forgotten. His lips feel warm and soft against mine, and then he kisses me harder, claiming my mouth with his, pushing mine open further. When I feel him flick his tongue against mine it makes my thighs quiver. We press into each other but then he pulls away, looking down at me with one of those inscrutable expressions.

'Sorry.'

Why is he sorry? That was amazing. But he's stepping away now and I feel suddenly bereft.

'Bye,' I say weakly, trying to process what has just happened.

'I'll see you soon,' he says, which could mean anything, though before he walks off I see him touch his mouth with his fingertips, as if he can't quite believe it either.

I watch him walk down the road, waiting for him to look back, but he doesn't. I let out the breath I didn't realise I had been holding and go in. Mum's in the kitchen and she looks at me and frowns.

'You didn't walk yourself home did you?'

'Mitch walked me,' I lie, not sure why but not wanting to tell Mum about Joe. For all that she worries about me not being interested enough in boys, I'm not sure he's someone she would approve of. Besides, I don't know what to make of him myself. My lips are still throbbing from the kiss, making me feel things low down in my body that I definitely don't want to discuss with her.

'Your dad phoned.'

I frown. He knew I was at Rianne's, he had dropped me there, so he must have phoned hoping to talk to Mum. I eye her suspiciously. She looks flushed, happy, though that could be because her work's going well.

'I'm going to bed,' I say, all of a sudden wanting to be alone. She just nods, looking distracted. Normally she would want to know all about my day, or question why I was going to bed so early.

'Night, baby.'

On impulse I give her a quick hug before going up to my room, and she ruffles my hair affectionately. I get upstairs and throw myself down on the bed, pushing thoughts of Mum and Dad to one side. I want to think about Joe. About the way his mouth felt on mine and that gorgeous body pressed against me...but then he had stepped away. Was I too full on? I think about the way I threw my arms around him and kissed him back, and blush. As if I do that with boys all the time, which is probably what he thinks now. I think of him telling Dean, of them discussing me in the way guys do, and it makes me cringe. I think about the way Adam and his friends had talked about Dannii. Joe seems more mature than that, but how would I know?

Remembering Adam and the way the other boy had grabbed me makes me feel icky. I'm lucky Joe came along when he did. Overwhelmed by the day's events I feel myself dropping off, a swirl of images in my mind. Rianne feeding the baby, my dad, Adam's sneering face and finally, Joe's mouth coming closer to mine, until they all blur into one and I fall asleep without even taking my coat off.

Chapter Three

The next morning, I'm at work. Poppy's is the only diner I know that opens on a Sunday, serving up roast dinners alongside its usual fare of breakfasts and burgers. It gets surprisingly busy. There's a couple of families in today as well as the usual people. I think the Sunday dinner thing is catching on.

I quite like working here, even though when I do the early mornings in the school holidays it gets hectic and I've been known to drop things or mix the orders up. But I love the friendly atmosphere and the banter with the customers. Today though I'm distracted, unable to stop my thoughts constantly turning back to last night and to Joe, and that kiss. My cheeks go hot and my tummy all fluttery every time I remember the way he leaned down and kissed me, and I've built the whole thing up to a big romantic scene in my mind that wouldn't be out of place in one of my novels. In romance stories though, the hero doesn't tend to abruptly pull away and walk home. I don't know what to make of it. He must like me, or why kiss me? But then, why apologise? I've been tormenting myself with it all morning.

'Damn.' I realise I'm burning the bacon and quickly get it onto the plate. If I arrange the beans carefully the customer won't notice the burnt bit, hopefully. I finish the rest of the breakfast, butter the toast and take it out to the old lady in the corner, who comes in every Sunday at lunchtime and orders an all-day breakfast. She smiles at me as I lay the plate in front of her and I feel bad about the bacon.

I'm behind the counter making a coffee when a voice makes me look up, startled.

'Ash.'

'Joe!' I nearly spill sugar all over myself. He grins at me as I wipe it off. 'What are you doing in here?'

'Came in for a burger.'

Oh. I try not to look disappointed, and I'm about to put on my best waitress voice and ask him what he would like to drink, and if he wants normal fries or curly ones, when he laughs.

'I'm joking, Ash. I came in to see you. Dean said you'd be here.'

I push the coffee over to the woman waiting for it and take the money without speaking. My heart is pounding. Get a grip, I tell myself. Shutting the till, I give Joe my full attention. He gives me a heart-breaking smile, and I see a little round dimple in his chin that I haven't noticed before. I feel an urge to kiss it.

'I wanted to say sorry for last night.'

This again. Is it his way of telling me he doesn't like me like that? I'm not one bit sorry, but I don't say anything, trying to look as if I'm not bothered one way or the other.

'I shouldn't have tried to kiss you after you had had a scare. I don't want you to think I was taking advantage.'

A scare? I realise he's talking about the guys harassing me at the park, and feel a rush of warmth towards him. How many eighteen-year-old boys worry about taking advantage? Generally, that's exactly what they're trying to do.

'It's okay,' I say, feeling a bit giddy. 'I didn't think you were.' I don't want to come right out and say, *I wanted you to kiss me, damn it*.

He looks pleased. We meet each other's eyes for a long moment, and I know I've got a goofy grin on my face but I can't seem to wipe it off, then I see my boss Becky looming behind him looking annoyed.

'Are you serving or what, Ash?' she says pointedly. Joe

quickly orders a coffee and she goes into the kitchen after throwing me a warning look. I grimace at Joe.

'Sorry, but she'll have a fit if I just stand here chatting. It'll be getting pretty busy soon.'

'That's okay. I wanted to ask you something.'

'Oh?' I pass him his coffee, wiping my hands on my apron and wishing I didn't look such a state. I've got a hairnet on and everything, to stop my unruly curls getting in anyone's food.

He looks down at his cup, and doesn't meet my eyes when he speaks.

'I was going to ask you if you wanted to go to the cinema Wednesday night. There's a new thriller out.'

He's asking me on a date! An actual date, not a casual meet up at Dannii's that could mean anything. An actual date.

'Uh, sure.' He looks as shocked by my acceptance as I am by his offer. We stare at each other, then grin simultaneously.

'Ash, some help please Becky calls from the kitchen and I roll my eyes. Joe laughs and I go in to help her, beaming. In fact, I can't wipe the smile off my face. Becky eyes me suspiciously. By the time I get back out Joe has gone, but there's a folded piece of paper next to his empty cup with my name on. His number. Grinning wide enough to split my face I slip it into my apron pocket. As soon as I've got a minute I'll text Dannii and see what she's doing later. I have to talk to someone about this.

She knows there's something up the minute I walk in. I'm still beaming, and she looks at me in surprise.

'What's up with you? Work couldn't have been that exciting.'

I smile mysteriously as I sit on the sofa. Or at least, I try to make it mysterious but I'm still grinning like a Cheshire cat so it probably doesn't have the desired effect. Dannii flops down next to me and looks at me impatiently. Her parents seem to be out, yet again. Sometimes I envy Dannii her freedom, but I can't imagine Mum being so blasé about what I'm up to.

'Have you seen Dean or Joe this weekend?' I ask, trying to prolong the suspense. Dannii raises an eyebrow.

'Dean, yes. Joe, no. Why?'

Unable to hold back any longer I launch into the full story, starting with my walk home from Rianne's and finishing with his impromptu visit to Poppy's this morning. I barely pause for breath, and I'm flushed and excited by the time I'm finished. But Dannii has a funny expression on her face. I was expecting squealing and suggestions for what to wear Wednesday, not an awkward silence.

'What?' I ask, sounding more than a touch defensive. Dannii looks down at her hands, then back up at me. She has a concerned look on her face, but something about it just doesn't ring true.

'It's just, are you sure you want to go out with him, Ash? I mean, he's hardly your type is he? And then there's the whole jail thing.'

I lean back, kind of shocked. I thought she would be excited for me, and since when does Dannii care about my 'type'? She's always trying to encourage me to go for boys more like the ones she goes for and okay, jail is pretty bad, but at least he's not a stoner like Dean. I don't say that to her though. Instead I give her Joe's version of the events that got him into trouble. Dannii just shrugs.

'He's not going to admit he's a complete thug is he? Especially when he's trying to get into your knickers.'

I scowl at her crude words and have to bite back the

retort that I'm not like her. In all honesty, the thought of Joe getting into said knickers fills me with as much excitement as it does nerves, but I don't say that to her either. The whole conversation just isn't going the way I expected it to, and there's an unspoken barrier between us that I don't understand.

'Is everything okay?' I ask, wondering if I've been too busy chattering about myself to notice Dannii might have problems of her own.

'Sure, babe.' She puts her hand on my knee. 'I'm just looking out for you. I don't want you to get mixed up in anything bad.'

I frown, remembering something Joe said as we were walking home.

'I thought you and Dean were trying to set me up with him? Isn't that why you invited me round the other night?'

Dannii gives this little laugh.

'Oh, that was Dean's idea. But I didn't actually expect the two of you to like each other.'

'Well, apparently we do.' I try to smile, but something about Dannii's whole attitude has put a dampener on my fizzing spirits. 'I've never had a date before, I thought you'd be giving me advice on clothes and what not to do on the back seat,' I joke. Dannii just gives a tight smile.

'Who actually goes on dates anymore anyway?' she says as if she's old hat at all this. 'He's probably just trying to take advantage, Ash, and knows you're a bit of a square.'

That's it, I'm pissed off. I glare at her, completely at a loss for a comeback, I'm so wrong-footed by her whole attitude, but she goes on relentlessly, as if she hasn't just totally insulted me. 'You're a virgin for God's sake, Ash. Do you really think he'll be interested when he realises you're a no go zone? I bet he's had loads of girls.'

That stings. Not least because the thought has crossed

my mind already.

'Not everything is about sex,' I snap, even though I know the feelings that Joe stirs up in me are a hell of a lot about sex, even if that is a subject I'm less than experienced in. Never before has Dannii thrown anything like this in my face, if anything she's always seemed quite proud of me. Perhaps she is just looking out for me.

'Maybe it's time I took the plunge.' The thought makes my heart race. With Joe? Maybe that is all he wants, isn't that the case with all teenage boys? But I think of the way he looked at me in the café earlier and don't want to believe it. If that's all he was after, why would he bother with a girl like me? As a challenge? The thought of him discussing me with Dean makes me feel sick.

'Well, I said yes to Wednesday,' I say, less certain of myself now. Dannii's face lights up in a sudden smile.

'I've got it, why don't we double date? Then I can suss out what he's up to, and you don't have to worry about him trying anything.' She looks pleased with herself.

'I don't know, I think he meant for it to just be the two of us,' I try to protest, but Dannii waves a hand airily.

'Don't be daft, it'll be much more fun. I'll text Dean now,' she whips her phone out of her pocket and I give a resigned sigh. She's just being a protective best friend after all, and I barely know Joe. He intimidated me at first, so maybe a double date isn't such a bad idea. Perhaps Dannii is, for once, being the sensible one.

'So what shall we wear?' she chirps, finally looking enthusiastic, and she pulls me into her room to raid her wardrobe. Dannii has tons of clothes, more than she will probably ever wear, which works out fine for me as I get to borrow loads of her stuff, although her tops are a lot looser around my boobs. We spend the next twenty minutes trying on various outfits, and she seems happy again.

'How are things with Dean?' I ask, wondering if that was why she was a bit short at first. She shrugs, holding a purple dress up to herself in the mirror. The colour looks great on her.

'Yeah, fine. He stayed over the other night.'

'Already?' I blurt out. After all, it's only been a few weeks. Dannii rolls her eyes at me as if I've just proven her earlier point and I blush, wondering if maybe I am a bit of a square after all. If Joe and I start dating, he's going to want to do more than just kiss. Dannii coming to the cinema with us is probably for the best, as I don't know how I would react to him trying to grope me in the dark. I really hope he wouldn't be that obvious, and if a guy behaved like that I'd usually be horrified, but at the same time my insides feel warm at the thought of Joe's hands anywhere on my body. I think about the way I practically threw myself at him last night. He affects me in a way I just haven't felt before. Surely Dannii doesn't feel that way about all of her boyfriends? I can't imagine Dean inspiring those feelings in anyone, but she must see something in him other than his car and a ready supply of weed. For the first time the differences between me and Dannii feel glaring. Well, maybe I'm sick of being a square. I hold up a white halter neck that Dannii has tried to get me in before that I've always discarded as too revealing.

'I'm wearing this,' I say firmly.

I change my mind by Wednesday of course, and settle for leggings and a tight yellow top that makes my hair and eyes pop. I get my mum to put some eye make up on me, as I always do my eyeliner squiggly or poke the mascara wand in my eye if I try to do it, and she looks almost as excited as me.

'So tell me all about him,' she asks, and I tell her he's a

friend of Dean's, a mechanic, and gorgeous. But nicer than Dean of course, because he doesn't smoke or seem to drink much.

I leave out the fact that he lives on the Estate, and has a criminal record, and that he faced off a gang of other boys without breaking a sweat. Mum looks so happy, and I don't want to burst her bubble. Or mine. I've been trying to push Dannii's words to one side all week, and just think about how Joe came to my rescue in the park, and then came to the diner just to ask me out. I've turned it into a novel worthy romance in my mind, and I really need to get a grip. If I'm not careful, I'll be doodling 'Ash loves Joe' all over my college books like a lovesick schoolgirl.

I've barely heard from him since Sunday, just a few texts, although I've been constantly checking my phone and driving myself crazy with it, even turning it off to stop myself from looking at it every two seconds and then rushing to turn it back on ten minutes later, in a total panic in case I've missed something. I just hope he doesn't mind too much about the whole double date thing; Dannii has pretty much taken over arrangements. She's picking me up with Dean and we're meeting Joe there. Even though it's still a date, it's dampened my excitement a bit, how am I supposed to get to know him with those two hanging around? But I tell myself not be mean; she's looking out for me after all, and it will make things less awkward.

I hear the car horn beep and grab my jacket, giving my mum a kiss on the cheek. She's wearing perfume. Taking a step back to look at her I realise she's a bit glammed up herself; her hair is in this complicated up do instead of her usual wild curls and I'm sure that her top is new. I've been too busy worrying about my own date to notice. I narrow my eyes at her suspiciously.

'Where are you off to?' I ask, as if I'm the parent.

'Just for a quick drink with the girls; I'll be back before you. Home by twelve, okay?'

I nod, but I'm not sure she's telling me the truth and that feels weird. Mum has never lied to me. Well, not since Santa Claus and the Tooth Fairy anyway.

A louder beep on the horn prevents me from saying anything else and I rush out, giving my hair a last ruffle in the hall mirror. Dannii's standing outside the passenger door to let me in – Dean's car is only a three door, a little Ford that always sounds on the verge of breaking down – and she looks amazing. A bit slutty, but amazing. Instead of the purple dress she's wearing the shortest denim skirt I've ever seen with an off the shoulder cropped top and some seriously high wedges. Her hair is down over her shoulders and I think she's wearing fake tan, which makes her legs all kind of shimmery and golden. A bit much for the cinema in April maybe, but there's no denying she looks great. Not so for Dean. As I get in the car he half leers half grins at me, and he's sporting a fluffy growth on his upper lip that might be trying to be a moustache. His eyes look slightly glazed, and I wish I had just got the bus. He's either had a beer or a joint, probably both, and I don't fancy being stopped by the police. Or crashing.

The whole way there he has one hand high on Dannii's leg, inching up her skirt, while she just giggles and gives him a knowing smile. They're definitely sleeping together, whereas I'm starting to feel I'm wearing my virginity like a flashing neon sign. And I bet virgins aren't Joe's normal type of girl, any more than he's my 'type' of boy.

Thinking about Joe makes my tummy flip, as if I can't wait to see him yet I'm dreading it all at once. I text him to let him know we're on our way, hoping he hasn't changed his mind. I've not heard from him since this morning; just a quick message to confirm the time. The day has been unbearably long, even though today was double history; my favourite class, much to Dannii's disgust. I spent lunch in the library as she had gone to see Dean on his dinner break. I think she likes him a hell of a lot more than I originally thought, and I don't know if that's a good thing or a bad.

Joe hasn't texted back, and as we turn into the parking lot of the cinema I scan it anxiously. What if he changes his mind? The thought grips me like a cold vice, but then I see him, waiting for us on the steps, and I want to get out of the car and go to him so bad I sit right on the edge of my seat, silently urging Dean to hurry up and park the car so I can get out. He walks over towards the car, looking straight through the window at me with the same boyish grin I've glimpsed before. In a plain white tee and jeans he doesn't look moody or intimidating anymore; he looks like a teenage heartthrob, straight out of one of Mum's old magazines from the nineties. When he avoids looking at Dannii clambering out of the car, all thighs and cleavage, I like him that little bit more.

'Hey,' he says, helping me out of the car and placing the lightest of kisses on my cheek, 'you look beautiful.'

I blush, murmuring my thanks. My cheek feels like it's burning where he kissed me. He looks at me intently and I wonder if he will kiss me again, properly this time, when Dannii puts herself in between us, throwing her arms around Joe and planting a loud kiss on his cheek. He steps back in surprise but she doesn't let go, and her boobs are crushed right up against his chest, nearly popping out of her top.

'Hi, babe,' she trills, as if Joe is some guy she's known for years. She's usually much cooler around boys. She notices me looking at her and steps away from Joe with a funny little laugh, winding her arm through Dean's and giving me a smug look over her shoulder. What is that all about? But I quickly forget about Dannii and her weird behaviour when Joe takes my hand as we walk in to the cinema.

He pays for my ticket and popcorn as well, waving my hand away when I reach for my purse. Dannii pays for Dean; I think she usually pays for his beer too. Dannii doesn't work, she just gets a generous allowance from her parents, so I guess it doesn't bother her too much. Still, I think it's a bit skanky of him.

We sit on the back row of course, with Dean at one end, me at the other and Joe and Dannii in the middle. She makes a fuss of sitting in between the two boys, and all through the trailers she seems to talk more to Joe than to Dean, leaning into him and touching his knee or shoulder. I don't know what point she's trying to make but she's definitely flirting, and she knows it. Dannii always has an agenda when she's around guys. Perhaps she wants to make Dean jealous. Either way I'd be getting pretty damn annoyed if it weren't for the fact that Joe seems to be completely oblivious to her charms. She finally gives up trying to involve him in conversation and turns to snogging Dean instead.

I'm acutely aware of Joe's proximity to me, and he feels even nearer when the lights dim. I can hear Dannii and Dean kissing, the rustle of clothes and her giving a breathy little moan. They're definitely making out, and when Joe's fingers brush mine I hold my breath, not knowing which will be worse, if he tries to touch me or if he doesn't. But all he does is lightly hold my hand, curling his fingers around mine. He looks at me and smiles shyly in the dim light, squeezing my hand. I squeeze back, unable to stop my eyes dropping to stare at those full lips. I want him to kiss me again, like he did on Saturday, but then the opening credits for the film come on and he settles back in his seat with his eyes fixed on the screen, though he doesn't let go of my hand. With his other arm, he nudges Dannii.

'The film's starting, lovebirds,' he says, and I detect a note of annoyance in his voice. Glancing over at them I see Dean remove his hand from within Dannii's skirt and lean back to watch the film with a smirk. Dannii digs in her rucksack and pulls out a four pack of beer, offering us one. I shake my head, glancing around to make sure there isn't an usher nearby but Joe takes one, and the pop of it opening sounds overloud as the music stops and the first scene begins. He takes a long swig and then places it in the drink holder in the arm of the chair and casually drapes his arm over so that his hand is on my knee. It's the gentlest touch rather than a typical boy grope and yet it sends a funny tingle up my leg that makes my inner thighs quiver. I should probably put my own hand on his leg, or at least hold his hand again but I sit frozen, aware only of the heat and weight of his palm on my leg just above my knee. Does he wish I had worn a skirt, like Dannii?

The film is a typical action movie, not my type of thing at all, and in any case I'm way too distracted by Joe to pay much attention to the screen though he seems engrossed in it. I wish Dannii was on the other side of me so we could have a giggle but she's too busy resuming her grope fest with Dean, though after a while she leans over Joe and waves a bottle at me. It's vodka.

'Want some, Ash? It might loosen her up a bit.' She winks at Joe, and I'm sure she's letting her cleavage brush against him on purpose. I shake my head, and I'm glad when Joe does too.

'Dean's driving,' he says to her pointedly. Dannii shrugs.

'More for us then.' She sits back, ignoring Joe's comment. He looks at me in concern.

'I'll walk you back.'

'Okay.' I nod, my heart leaping at the thought of getting some time on my own with him and then sinking again as I see Dannii passing Dean the bottle and knowing there's no way I can let her get in a car he's driving. I've never known her to be this irresponsible.

Joe's hand is still on my knee and after a few minutes he begins to move his fingertips in little circles, massaging the inside of my knee cap. It feels nice, and somehow as intimate as anything Dannii and Dean are getting up to next to us. I still really, really want him to kiss me again. His hand moves further up my thigh, moving in circles, squeezing the fleshy bits on the inside of my leg through my leggings. My leg feels hot under his touch, and my mouth has gone dry. When his hand stops its travelling and settles near the top of my thigh I let out a breath I didn't know I had been holding, just as Joe leans over and brushes my lips with his.

'You taste of popcorn,' he whispers, flicking the tip of his tongue across my lower lip.

'You taste of beer,' I whisper back, and go to do the same to his lip but he puts his mouth over mine fully and before I know it we're kissing properly, his other hand sliding around my back and pulling me into him so that the arm of the chairs separating us pushes into my tummy. It should be uncomfortable, but I really don't care. He moves the hand on my leg up into my hair, burying it in my curls as he pulls back to nibble on my lower lip. He pulls away smiling, leaving me feeling dazed.

'You're a great kisser, Ash.'

'Thanks.' I don't know what else to say to that, it's not as if I've had much practice. I didn't think about what I was doing either, it just felt natural, as if there's no reason for me to be doing anything else in the world apart from kissing Joe.

He takes my hand again and sits back, and I lean in closer to him, feeling happy.

'I don't know what's going on now,' he says, motioning at the screen. Dannii, who must have taken a break from snogging the face off Dean, hears him and laughs.

'I wouldn't ask, Ash, she's not interested in anything that happens unless it was at least five hundred years ago are you babe? Total history geek.'

Although she says the last bit with affection, I feel stung at her comment, but before I can say anything Joe jumps to my defence.

'Don't blame her. It's why I like cars so much, they're easier to deal with than real people.' He squeezes my hand again and I smile at him gratefully. I suppose he's right too, it is a way of escaping. Funny how he's made it sound like our very different interests are actually something we have in common. I give Dannii a smug look but unfazed she takes another swig of vodka and turns back to Dean.

The two of them get louder as the film goes on, with Dannii letting out mock-offended squeals and Dean laughing loudly. I see his hands disappearing into her bra and Dannii making a loud show of slapping them away without actually removing them. In the row in front of us an older guy turns round and shushes us angrily. Dean leans forward like he's about to say something, then sees Joe glaring at him and sits back, mumbling. They're quiet for a while, then start up again just as the film's gearing up to its climax. Annoyed tutting comes from the row behind us and Dannii sticks her two fingers up without removing her face from Dean's neck. I bury my head in Joe's shoulder in embarrassment.

'I'm sorry,' I groan. He kisses the top of my head.

'It's not your fault, but I thought this would happen

when you said they were coming.'

'It was Dannii's idea.'

'Really?' He gives me a sideways glance. 'She said it was yours. I thought you were worried about being on your own with me.'

He sounds almost hurt and I glare at Dannii over his shoulder, not that she notices. I'll get no sense out of her now, she must have had at least half of that bottle of vodka.

'I wanted to be on my own with you,' I say quietly, then wince at how it sounds. Still, he looks pleased.

I'm glad when the end credits roll and we can get out of there. People walking past from the rows in front glare at us and I duck my head in embarrassment when Dannii trips over the seats, laughing at something only she finds funny.

'She needs to go home, she's wasted,' I say to Joe, but Dannii puts her hands on her hips and glares at me, her eyes unfocused.

'I'm going home with Dean. Staying at his. Aren't I?' she nudges Dean, who nods and walks out of the cinema unsteadily, Dannii at his heels. I turn to Joe in despair.

'He can't drive her like that.'

'I know,' he sighs, following them out. I catch up with Dannii, trying to reason with her. She could get her parents to come pick her up, or maybe I should ring my dad.

'At least get a cab,' I plead with her, but she shakes her head mutinously like a naughty toddler. She'll be stamping her feet in a minute.

'It's all right,' Joe calls. He's standing by the car with Dean. 'I've got the keys, I'll drive.'

'You're not on my insurance,' Dean protests. Joe rolls his eyes at him. 'No, but at least I'm sober. I've had one beer, how many have you had?'

Dean looks like he's giving serious thought to that

question, then he gives in and gets in the back of the car. Dannii follows him, giving me a furious look. I just ignore her, but if I'm honest I really feel as if she's let me down. She's ruined the night, our first date. She could have got drunk with Dean anywhere.

I get in the car and buckle up, looking over at Joe, who looks grim.

'I'll drop these two off first, then you,' he says without looking at me.

'What about the car?'

'Dean can come and get it before he goes to work tomorrow. Walk his hangover off.'

I glance at Dean lolling in the back seat. I hope the pool hall doesn't open too early in the morning, because I doubt he'll be fit for anything. He must have been drinking before he picked me up too. Mum would go mad if she knew. At least I should be getting in before her; it's still only ten.

Joe drives in silence, his hands tense on the wheel, constantly checking his mirrors as if he's worried about being pulled over.

'You'll be okay. You've only had one drink,' I try to reassure him, but he just shakes his head angrily and I shrink back, wondering if I've done something wrong.

By the time we pull up outside Dean's the anger is rolling off him in waves. He practically hauls Dean out of the car and although he helps Dannii out he steps back so quickly when she tries to hug him that I'm surprised she doesn't fall on her face. Too drunk to care she blows me a kiss through the window.

'Bye, babe, I'll call you tomorrow. Make sure you get her home safe,' she says to Joe, wagging her finger at him as Dean pulls her into his house. He shares with three other guys, so at least they don't have to worry about angry parents.

'That's rich coming from her,' Joe huffs as he pulls away. It's the first time he's spoken since we left the cinema.

'You seem angry,' I state the obvious. He glances at me in concern.

'Not with you. Just Dean getting in that state. If we had got pulled over…I'm on probation, Ash, and those two are as high as kites and I bet Dean's got weed on him, maybe worse.'

I hadn't thought of that. Perhaps Dean isn't so harmless after all. He certainly doesn't seem to be doing Dannii any good.

'Yet you drove us home anyway. That's twice you've rescued me now,' I smile at him, and finally he looks a bit more relaxed.

'You're turning out to be pretty high maintenance, Ash,' he chuckles. Feeling daring, I put a hand on his knee. He puts his hand briefly over mine before he has to change gears and his touch sends a jolt through me. I squeeze his leg, feeling the firmness and width of his lower thigh, before putting my hand back in my lap, my heart racing.

'Did you have a girlfriend before you were in jail?' I ask, curious but at the same time almost not wanting to know. He hesitates, then nods.

'Yeah, but she didn't want to know afterwards. I can't say I blame her. I let everyone down.' He looks angry again and I wish I hadn't mentioned it. There are so many things I want to know about him, but I don't want to seem like I'm prying. To my horror I spend the next few minutes silently seething with jealousy about his girlfriend, and wondering if she was prettier or cooler or smarter than me. Probably all three. And definitely not a virgin.

He must have read my mind, or at least sensed an atmosphere, because he leans over and squeezes my knee in a way that seems more affectionate than sexual.

'I got over her ages ago. It would never have worked out.'

I nod and mumble something non-committal, trying not to seem too interested. *Please don't ask me,* I pray, wishing I had never opened this particular can of worms, but of course he does.

'How about you, no recent exes?'

'Erm, no, not recent.' I clear my throat, deciding not to bother lying because no doubt Dannii would have filled him in anyway. 'In fact not any, really.'

He takes his eyes off the road for a moment to glance at me with that unreadable expression I'm quickly becoming familiar with.

'That's good,' he says blandly, and I have no idea what he means. Good as in *good because I like you and I don't want any rivals* or good as in *oh my God she's even more inexperienced than I thought but I'd better be polite*?

'Why do you live with your aunt?' I blurt out in a desperate attempt to change the subject and then mentally kick myself for being way too nosy yet again. He's quiet for a few moments as he turns the car into my neighbourhood and when he speaks it's in a monotone, as if he's reciting answers.

'I haven't seen my dad in years and my mum's dead. Cancer.'

'I'm sorry.' Now I feel awful, and at the same time want to throw my arms round him. I can relate to a father not being around but the thought of anything happening to my mum makes me feel ill. All of a sudden I just want to go home and hug her, before remembering she's probably not in.

As Joe pulls up at the end of my road I sit in silence, willing him to say something and wishing I had never asked about either his past girl or his parents. What with Dannii's antics and now my clumsy prying, my first ever real date has been kind of a disaster.

Or maybe not. I unclip my belt and go to say 'bye' when he reaches for me, not in a lungey grabby way but carefully as if he thinks I'm fragile or something, stroking my cheek and then sliding his hand round the back of my neck. He leans over and my heart starts pounding as I realise he's going to kiss me again. I've been waiting for this all night yet now I just sit frozen, staring at his mouth as it comes towards me in what feels like slow motion. I don't want to throw myself at him again so when his lips touch mine I barely respond, but when his warm mouth encloses mine and his hand tightens on the back of my neck I let out a little gasp before I start kissing him back as if my lips and tongue have a will of their own.

We kiss for what feels like ages, and then I feel his other hand creeping up my ribcage. Somehow we're now nearly lying back across the seats with him over me, his hip wedged into my thigh. It's slightly uncomfortable and I turn, which brings his hand up right under my breast. I freeze, having a moment's panic that he's going to try and grope me, but he slides his hand around my breast up to my collarbone, and then down a little again, then around again, but without actually touching me.

Which makes me want him to. I arch my back, almost pushing my chest into his hand but he slides it down and away again, breaking away from the kiss to nibble at my lower lip. It's so lovely and so weirdly frustrating all at once that I nip him back with a little more force.

'Easy, tiger.' He laughs, my breath warm on his neck. He kisses me again and shifts his weight, and I can feel just how turned on he is through his jeans. Almost in wonder and hardly believing my own daring, I reach down and brush my hand between us, rubbing my palm over the bulge in his pants. Joe gasps and moves his hips away.

'Ash, don't, I'll embarrass myself,' he whispers in my ear, and I blush, realising just what he means. I scramble to sit up, not quite believing what I've just done, and straighten my top. My hands are trembling. He just sits there looking at me with a funny little smile on his face.

'What?' I ask, defensive.

'You're so hot,' he says, and grins when I blush again, though inside there's a little cheerleader shaking her pom poms. He thinks I'm hot! We sit and grin at each other for a few more minutes before I get out, nearly tripping because my legs are shaky.

'I'll see you tomorrow?'

'Sure,' I respond, which would sound a lot cooler if I wasn't still grinning like I want to split my face. He gives me a little wave as he drives off and I practically run into my house. The dog bounces up to me with his tongue lolling and tail wagging, picking up on my mood.

I start to fix a sandwich, still thinking about Joe's mouth and hands on me and the 'hot' comment, when Mum comes in from the door as fast as I did, looking like she's just been laughing. I wave at her before it hits me that her hair is all mussed up and she's got a silly grin on her face. Just like me, walking in after kissing Joe. I go past her into the hall and open the front door to see a car driving away that looks a lot like my dad's. I crane my neck trying to see the number plate when Mum comes up behind me and takes the door, ushering me in.

'Hurry up, it's cold.'

'Who were you out with again?' I ask and she narrows her eyes at me.

'Don't question me, young lady, I should be asking you that. How did your date go anyway?'

She's changing the subject on purpose, I just know it. My good mood deflated, I don't want to talk to her about Joe, not even the good bits.

'It was fine,' I shrug. Mum looks disappointed and ruffles my hair, then goes into the kitchen. Normally I'd be getting twenty questions.

'Night then,' I say, and she turns and beams at me and offers her cheek for a kiss, but I know I'm right; there's something going on. I hope it's not Dad, I really do, but I don't want to ask. Upstairs I take off my make-up, brush my teeth and throw myself on the bed, wanting to think about Joe but still worrying about Mum when my phone beeps. It's him.

Home now. Nite gorgeous.

And that's all it takes to put the smile back on my face.

Chapter Four

Joe, Joe, Joe. He's all I can think about, to the point that instead of taking notes in Sociology I'm doodling hearts and not very good flowers on the edge of the page, resisting temptation to scribble 'Ash loves Joe'. I'm not fourteen anymore.

'Ashley?'

I look up, puzzled, to see the teacher looking at me in bemusement and the rest of the class staring at me expectantly and realise he's just asked me a question I didn't even hear. Flushing, I desperately rack my brains to remember anything he's said in the last five minutes, before he saves me any more embarrassment and moves on to someone else. The boy I'm sitting next to, Dwayne, looks at me and mouths, 'are you okay?' looking seriously concerned as if I might have a terminal illness or something. I just nod and cover my page with my arm, but he has already glanced at the hearts and looks away with a little smirk. I feel horribly exposed, and half turn my back to him. I like Dwayne and often eat lunch with him, but I'm not ready to share Joe just yet. Not even with Dannii, or perhaps least of all with her given her behaviour last night. She's not in today, no doubt nursing a serious hangover.

This is different to any of my schoolgirl crushes; after all, something has actually happened. Every time I think of that, of his hand creeping up my ribcage and my own clumsy and curious fumbling, a warm melting feeling starts in my belly and spreads through my whole body. I'm on hyper alert lately, as if all my senses have been heightened. As much as it's a kind of nice feeling – nice being a totally inadequate description, but I can't seem to find anything that describes it – it's also uncomfortable and totally unfamiliar. Did I say that I love being in love? Well maybe now that I'm actually getting some hands-on experience I'm not so sure.

The class ends with me having learned precisely nothing, and I'm so used to being a bit of a class nerd that I feel guilty and a bit disorientated, like the time I cut class with Dannii and Rianne and spent the whole two hours fretting about what I was missing. Well, it was exam year.

I find my usual seat in the library and fire up my laptop, intending to do some research for that history essay which I still haven't completed, and instead logging straight on to Facebook, wondering if Dannii has posted anything about last night. Seeing the icon flashing that shows I've got a friend request, I click on it and draw a sharp breath. Joe. It's a grainy picture taken on a not very good phone by the look of it, but it's unmistakably him, those piercing eyes and that lush mouth. *The mouth I've kissed.* The thought sends a tingle through me. I accept it and go straight to his page to have a look. There's only the one picture of him; it looks as though he only joined a few hours ago. Instantly I look at his friends list and see only a few people; with a sigh of relief I see they're mostly boys. The thought of Joe sitting on the computer talking to other girls makes me queasy. I wonder if his ex is on here. I send him a quick message to say hi and then log off before I can drive myself crazy. Jealousy isn't something I've ever experienced over a guy before and I'm amazed at how it feels; a sick, crawly feeling but also angry, like I want to hit something. Insane.

Insane or not, it bugs me all afternoon and I can't concentrate on anything, it's like I'm ill or something. As I'm walking home I debate with myself whether or not I should text him, then remember he will be at work, which raises the question of whose computer he was using. He didn't seem at all interested in talking to me online when I mentioned it last week. Perhaps he's met other girls he wants to talk to as well.

In the end I ring Dannii, who answers the phone sounding sorry for herself.

'Urgh, I feel rotten,' she whimpers. 'Dean didn't go to work this morning either.'

That doesn't surprise me. Dean is a future candidate for a trashy talk show if ever I saw one.

'Are you still at his house, then?'

'No, I came home earlier. My brother's here; his girlfriend kicked him out.'

Dannii's brother Michael is an older version of her; spoilt and a bit selfish yet everyone adores him. Totally gorgeous too, though I've never really been able to look at him like that. I can remember him at primary school trying to look up the girls' skirts.

'Joe's on Facebook. I spoke to him earlier.'

I feel another sharp pang of jealousy in my gut. He must have been on there talking to Dannii before I had even gone online.

'Wasn't he at work?'

'Yeah, he said he was on the laptop in the office. It must have been quiet; I was talking to him for about twenty minutes.'

Another pang, sharper this time.

'Did he mention me?'

She pauses.

'Not much. He did say to tell you he'd phone you when he finishes.'

My heart drops at her first words then leaps at the last.

'Did he say what time?' I ask in a rush, eager now, and Dannii just laughs.

'You have got it bad haven't you?' she teases.

'Shut up,' I protest, but it makes me smile.

We wrap up the conversation by agreeing to meet up later, although if I'm honest, if Joe wants to see me again tonight I would rather Dannii and Dean weren't there, and not just because of last night's drunken antics. I want to be on my own with him.

When I get home there's no sign of Mum, just a note by the fridge.

Gone out, won't be back late, call me if you need anything. There's stew in the pot. DO NOT walk home on your own.

This is seriously weird. I mean okay, she does go out occasionally, but not without telling me where she's going, even if just in passing. She's hiding something, and I've got a sinking feeling I know exactly what it is. On impulse I pick up the house phone and call my dad without knowing quite what I'm going to say.

'Where are you?' I blurt out as soon as he picks up. He immediately sounds worried.

'Ash? Is everything okay?'

'Er, yeah. I was just wondering if you wanted to do something tonight?'

There's an uncomfortable pause before he answers.

'I'm a bit busy tonight, Princess, how about tomorrow?'

Busy with Mum? I want to ask, but don't. I could be wrong, or even worse, I could be right. I know most kids with divorced parents would be happy if they thought their parents might get back together, but I'm not. I'm not a kid anymore for a start and it's way too late for him to come swanning back into my life on a full time basis. I'll be off to uni next year, and where will that leave Mum when he breaks her heart again?

But I don't say any of this.

'Fine, I'll see you tomorrow,' I snap. 'And please stop calling me Princess.' I slam the phone down before he can answer and storm upstairs. After fuming at the wall for twenty minutes I ring Dannii again, but she sounds distracted and doesn't understand why I'm so bothered.

'They're grown-ups, Ash, let them get on with it. Anyway they'll be so busy with each other she won't ask too many questions about Joe. Your mum won't approve of him you know.' She says the last bit with relish, as if she almost can't wait for the anticipated drama. I murmur something non-committal and let her go, feeling a bit lost. I need someone to talk to and if it's not Mum or Dannii, then who else is there? I don't want to ring Rianne in case she's busy with the baby and my class friends are more like homework buddies, not people I can pour my heart out to. On an impulse, I phone Joe. He picks up on the second ring.

'Babe!' He greets me warmly and I feel instantly a bit better, unable to stop myself smiling even though I was so upset a moment before.

'Hi.' I realise I have no idea what to say and there's a silence before he speaks, and he sounds hesitant, almost shy, like on Sunday when he came to the café to ask me out.

'I was wondering if you wanted to come round mine tonight? I could meet you from work?'

He's inviting me to his house? Wow.

'Will your aunt be there?'

'Sure, but don't worry, she won't ask you a million questions or anything.'

I'm not sure if I'm relieved or disappointed that we won't be completely alone, but I am curious to both see his house and meet his aunt. Remembering how self-conscious he seemed about where he lived, I feel strangely flattered.

'I'd love to.'

'Great. I'll meet you across from the park at six. I might be a bit oily from work.'

'Oily's great,' I say, imagining him in his greasy overalls

and not a lot else and feeling glad he can't see me blush down the phone.

As we say bye I look at the clock and groan when I see I've got nearly two hours to wait. Two hours to tie myself up in knots thinking about him and worrying about Mum. I try to eat some of the stew she's left, but even though it's delicious my stomach's churning too much to eat. The next two hours feel like the longest of my life.

'So you're Ashley? Aren't you gorgeous?'

His aunt, a small round woman, older than I was expecting but with a smile that takes ten years off her, greets me with so much warmth I take a step back in surprise, though it's impossible not to grin back.

'Leave her alone, Steph,' he protests, winking at me and rolling his eyes. He hugs her with obvious affection, which surprises me, as most lads I know would find it horribly embarrassing. There are so many different sides to Joe he puzzles me, but seeing how relaxed he looks I've got no doubt this is very much the real him.

'I'm just going for a quick shower,' he says, grimacing down at his oily work overalls, which I personally think make him look sexy as hell. 'Don't let her terrorise you.'

His aunt swats at him playfully with her tea towel as he heads upstairs and ushers me onto a stool by the little breakfast bar. It's a small house, a terraced two up two down that's typical of the houses in this area, but it's sparklingly clean and tastefully decorated. It's not what I was expecting, and I feel a bit ashamed for making assumptions. Oblivious to my discomfort Steph chats away as she makes coffee, bombarding me with so many questions about classes, family etc. that I barely have time to answer them before she's on to the next. So much for Joe's assurances. Then she's staring at me expectantly, and I can't for the life of me remember what she's just said.

'Er, sorry?' I ask, feeling stupid. I'm so scatter brained lately.

'I said Joe really likes you. I haven't seen him this happy since he was released.'

I get a warm, fuzzy glow at her words, but I'm surprised she mentioned his time in jail. It gives me an opening to ask a few questions of my own.

'Was he there long?'

She tilts her head and looks at me as if she's sizing me up, then gives a little nod as if she's decided something. I feel oddly like I've passed some kind of test.

'Only a few months; he got out on good behaviour. If you ask me, he shouldn't have been there in the first place. But he took it quite hard; feels like he's let everyone down.'

I nod, thinking of the guarded way he gets when I ask him questions about it.

'So you're his mum's sister?'

Steph chuckles, which makes her cheeks and chin wobble. She's plump, but in that healthy looking way that suits some people, like you just couldn't imagine them skinny; it wouldn't look right.

'I'm her aunt, actually, Joe's great-aunt, but sweet of you to assume otherwise. Joe was very close to Gayle – his mother – and it did sent him off the rails a little, poor lamb.'

I can't help smiling at her calling Joe a 'poor lamb'. It doesn't quite fit his cool guy image. If Dean or Dannii were here they'd tease him about it for days.

I want to ask her more about his background when I hear him behind me and turn round on the stool quickly, as if I've been caught out.

He's naked. Well, okay, maybe not quite but he may as well be judging by the blush that starts with my face and warms me all the way down to my chest. He's wearing nothing but a white towel round his waist, and only one thought comes to my head. *Wow.* Still damp from the shower, his hair wet and slicked back so that it looks darker, making his eyes look even more intense than usual, and *oh my God that body...*Every inch of him is tanned and toned to perfection, and he's got the body of a man, not a boy. I swallow, my mouth too dry to speak. Joe winks at me as if he knows exactly what I'm thinking.

'Put some clothes on,' Steph says. 'You're not taking the poor girl upstairs like that.'

Joe grins.

'I've got shorts on. You coming up, Ash?' He holds his hand out to me and I take it, a tingle going up my arm as we touch. I slide off the stool and follow him upstairs, my hand still in his.

'No funny business!' Steph calls up after us and Joe chuckles low in his throat. Although I know she's downstairs and he's not likely to try anything, it feels deliciously – yet nerve-rackingly – wicked to be going into the bedroom of a half-naked boy, being led by the hand. I feel like a blushing virgin from one of my novels. Let's face it, I am a blushing virgin.

A sudden thought occurs to me; does Joe know? He should do, after all I told him I'd never had a proper boyfriend, but that doesn't always matter. I know plenty of girls my age who lost their virginity at parties or in the local park to guys they barely know. Dannii's one of them. Rianne too; although thankfully for the baby, they actually fell in love and stayed together. The thought of just doing that with anyone makes me feel a bit queasy, and I'm hoping Joe has realised that about me and isn't expecting any level of experience from me. Then I remember my hand reaching for his crotch in the car. What if he thinks I carry on like that with every boy who tries to kiss me? Not that there's been that many, of course.

As we reach his room he must sense my hesitation because he stops and turns to me, looking concerned.

'Don't think I'm bringing you up here to get into your underwear or anything. I just thought we could chill.'

I nod, squeezing his hand, and he leads me into his room.

It's a typical boy's room; posters of cars and girls, a stack of car magazines – I can't help wondering if he's hiding a porn stash in them – and a pile of CDs and DVDs next to a small TV and stereo. No fancy plasma or array of the latest gadgets, but there is a small weight bench with a pair of dumb bells on the floor. There's a picture of a woman on the wall; pretty, with the same colour hair and eyes as Joe. His mum.

The only other thing that strikes me as different is how clean his room is, almost military. The bed is made without a crease and the pile of magazines are in a perfect stack, not all thrown on top of each other like my books. I wonder if it's a jail thing, or if he's always been like this.

'Want some music on?' he asks, and I nod, flicking through his CDs and choosing a band I like that aren't too cheesy. He puts it on, then unwraps the towel to reveal he is indeed wearing shorts, if you can call them that. White and tight, he looks like a catalogue model, and as he turns to pull on a pair of jeans I can't help staring at his butt. To my disappointment he pulls the jeans on quickly and then a t-shirt too, spoiling my view.

He flops down on the bed next to me and reaches for a lock of my hair, twirling it between his fingers.

'It's a beautiful colour.'

'What, ginger?' I scoff. I've always been a bit self-conscious about my hair. It's not ginger, not exactly, but there's enough red in it that I was teased mercilessly in junior school until Dannii stepped in on my behalf.

'It's more of an auburn,' Joe says, still playing with it. 'It's pretty.'

No one's ever called my hair pretty before, least of all the hottest boy I've ever seen. I smile down at him, feeling the urge to lean down and kiss that lush mouth, still pink and damp from his shower. He pulls me down so I'm practically on top of him and kisses the tip of my nose, then stares intently at me until I fidget and look away.

'I really like you, Ash. Honestly, I've never met a girl like you before.'

I shift uncomfortably. 'I'm nothing special,' I protest, and even as I say it I think how true it is, how I can't fathom what he sees in me. Joe shakes his head at me, looking cross.

'Don't say that. You're so pretty, so clever. You're way out of my league.'

I cough and almost choke, I'm so surprised at his words. Me, out of his league? He really has been locked up too long. He might just be saying it so he can get his way of course, like most boys, but looking at him I feel instinctively that he means it.

'I really like you too,' I say shyly. What an understatement. 'Like' doesn't even come close to describing the way I feel about him. 'Lust' definitely. 'Obsession' possibly. 'Love'? it's too soon for that surely, but I can't deny the fluttery, excited feeling I get when I think about him or know I'm going to see him, or the crazy jealousy I felt earlier in the library. For a minute I wonder if I should mention what Dannii had said about their conversation on Facebook, then I hear my phone ringing. Right on cue, it's Dannii.

'Damn, I forgot, I told her we might meet up with them,'

I tell Joe as I put the phone to my ear. He rolls his eyes as if he can't think of anything worse.

'Where are you?' Dannii asks. She sounds excited, and there are voices and music in the background.

'I'm at Joe's,' I say a touch smugly, expecting her to squeal with interest and ask a dozen questions, but she just pauses and then carries on as if I hadn't even spoken.

'Michael's got some friends round, we're having a bit of a party; you have to come.'

'I've got classes tomorrow.'

'Oh, stop being such a bore. You don't have to stay long. Bring Joe; Dean's here and some other guys he knows, I think.'

I sigh and look at Joe, who's sitting close enough to hear. He shrugs.

'If you want.'

I cover the mouthpiece with my hand.

'I did tell her we'd go round or something. Maybe we could just go for an hour?'

I tell Dannii I'll see her soon and ring off. I look at Joe, wondering if he's pissed off but he's smiling at me and pulling me gently towards him.

'We'll go in five minutes,' he whispers as his arms go round me. His mouth closes on mine, and I'm lost.

Twenty minutes of frenzied snogging later that leaves me hot and flustered, waking up parts of my body I don't want to talk about, and we're on our way to Dannii's. His arm is slung casually around me as if it belongs there. I like that feeling more than I want to admit to. I feel proud to be on his arm, and not just proud in an 'I'm so cool look at my hot boyfriend way'. Proud like I want to be his.

Michael flings open the door and looks me up and down with a leer, letting out a low whistle.

'Well, look who's all grown up,' he drawls, running his eyes over my hips and boobs. Joe steps slightly in front of me and holds his hand out to Michael, who slaps it in that boy way that passes for a handshake.

'I'm Joe, Ashley's boyfriend.' There's no mistaking the unspoken warning tone to his voice. Michael's mouth makes a little 'oh' of surprise, and he steps aside to let us in, keeping his eyes firmly away from my boobs. I'm grinning to myself, mostly because he described himself as my 'boyfriend'.

There's already a group of people in the kitchen, mostly boys I don't recognise, and bottles of beer lined up on the side. Their parents must be out of town. Again. I've asked Dannii before if they know or care what she gets up to when they're not here, and she just shrugged. 'Not as long as the house is clean.' Sometimes I feel sorry for her. Mum might not have the money to buy me every new dress and gadget I want, but at least she's interested. Even my dad tries his best, I suppose. Still, I don't want to think about them and what they may or may not be doing might now.

'Babe!'

Dannii sashays up to me, grabbing me in a perfumed hug and kissing me on the cheek with sticky glossed lips. She looks great as usual in hot pants and a long tee and I wish I'd gone home to get changed before coming. I glance at Joe over her shoulder and see him looking at her legs. My enthusiasm dampened I wriggle out of Dannii's embrace and grab myself a beer, popping the top with my teeth and taking a long swig. It tastes foul.

'Looks like you're making a bad girl out of her,' Dannii quips to Joe, who looks at me intently. I take another swig.

'You not having one?' I say, flipping my hair in a Dannii-like manner. Joe reaches for a beer, frowning at me.

'You okay?'

'Sure. Let's go dance.'

I wander into the front room, taking another swig of beer and telling myself to get a grip. Being around Joe opens up such a tangled box of emotions I can't seem to sort through them all. I go over to Dean by the iPod docker, who is clearly acting as DJ, and start swaying to the music. I can't really dance, but all Dannii ever does is this hip swaying thing and it seems to work for her.

'Nice ass,' I hear behind me and I turn round, half expecting Jake but coming face to face with a boy I immediately recognise. It's Jason, the ringleader from the park. He looks surprised as he recognises me, then smirks.

'We meet again.'

'Hi,' I say cockily, feeling braver in a room full of people with Dean to one side and Joe in the other room talking to Dannii. Why is he still talking to Dannii? I crane my neck over Jason's shoulder to see into the kitchen but there's no sign of either of them, only Michael talking to a girl with pink hair. He catches my eye and winks at me. 'Where's Dannii?' I mouth but he's already turned away to carry on his conversation. I turn back to Jason, who's still looking at me, and there's something predatory in his gaze that makes me step back, closer to Dean.

'Hey, man,' he says to Jason casually. Somehow it doesn't surprise me that Dean knows him. Dean is the kind of middle class wannabe thug that would find idiots like Jason cool. I bet he wouldn't be so friendly if he had heard the comments Jason and Adam were making about Dannii in the park. I look at Dean making 'help me!' eyes, but as usual he's oblivious to anything that's going on. Not for the first time I wonder what the hell Dannii is doing with him.

'Feeling a bit friendlier today?' Jason smirks at me, ignoring Dean. I swallow, all my cockiness gone. Out of all the guys I know, it should be Jason that's been to prison, because there's an air of barely repressed nastiness about him that probably makes old ladies cross the street to avoid him. Hell, after that incident at the park, I'd cross the street to avoid him.

'I'm fine,' I try to say in a snotty voice but it comes out as more of a frightened squeak. Jason steps forward and I visibly flinch, but he's only leaning into Dean to talk about tunes. Seeing my cue to escape I decide to go and talk to Michael, then I see Joe coming towards us. Danni isn't far behind him, her face slightly red.

'What's this idiot doing here?' Joe stands next to me, glowering at Jason, who glowers back but looks a lot less sure of himself. He shoots a look over his shoulder at two equally sulky looking boys slouching near the sofa who immediately stand to attention, no doubt poised in case he needs back up. Trust Dannii to let just anyone into her house.

'I invited him,' Dannii says looking puzzled. 'What's the problem?'

'He tried to grope Ashley in the park. Get him out of here. Before I do.' Joe speaks quietly, but through gritted teeth, never taking his eyes off Jason, who squares up to him as if he's about to hit him. Joe doesn't move. The two cronies near the sofa sidle a bit closer.

Dannii looks at Joe, at Dean, who looks confused, and then turns towards the kitchen and waves urgently at Michael, who walks over with a frown on his face, just as Jason's two friends come right up behind him, making a perfect trio of teen boot camp candidates.

'They're causing trouble,' Dannii says firmly, and Michael nods. He might be laid back and a bit of a joker, but he's also a few years older than us and well-built. Standing next to Joe, they look more than a match for Jason and his little crew.

'Out,' Michael says firmly. Jason nods at his friends to indicate it's time to leave, but not before shooting Joe a threatening look.

'Later,' he says. Joe raises an eyebrow. They're doing that secret macho code, where few words are spoken but they each know what the other means. Of course if they were girls there would probably be a screaming match followed by an emotional make friends in the toilets. This though, feels serious and as I watch Jason beating a hasty retreat I feel worried for Joe. I snuggle into him, feeling cold and he kisses the top of my head tenderly. Dannii looks at me with a funny expression on her face.

'Where did you go?' I ask. In the weird exchange with Jason I had forgotten I was looking for them.

'Toilet,' Joe says curtly. Dannii just looks away. I feel a horrible pang of apprehension. *But where were you?* I think, but she's started berating Dean for not getting rid of Jason earlier.

'You invited them,' he says defensively.

Dannii just rolls her eyes as if he's the most useless person she's ever met, then turns to me, saying brightly, 'C'mon, Ash, lets go have some fun!' Linking her arm through mine she makes her way back to the kitchen.

'Want some? Mum left it.' She waves a bottle of expensive wine in my face. I shrug. The only time I've ever drank wine it made me feel sick, but it's a party and I'm sick of her calling me a bore.

It actually tastes quite nice and I gulp it back, making Dannii giggle.

'Careful, babe, it's not pop.'

'Didn't know you like wine,' Joe says behind me, giving Dannii a disapproving glance. Feeling mellower I lean back against his chest, relaxing as his arms go around me. I decide I'm being silly worrying about him and Dannii; he doesn't even seem to like her very much.

Dannii starts dancing with Dean, grinding her hips into him. He grabs her butt, winking at Joe. I can't see Joe's face and turn my head to look at him. He snatches a kiss, taking me by surprise. I turn round into his arms and kiss him back, darting my tongue between his teeth. I'm more confident about kissing him now, as if I've been kissing him on a daily basis for months. He makes a sound like a growl low in his throat, pulling me tighter into him.

'Let's leave the lovebirds alone,' I hear Dean say, and he pulls Dannii out of the kitchen, pulling the door nearly shut behind them. I run a hand through Joe's hair. Just like last night in the car I can feel his erection through his trousers and shamelessly push my groin into his. It feels so good I can't help wondering how he would feel inside me. Would it hurt? Just as I have the thought Joe breaks away from our kiss and says softly,

'You're a virgin aren't you?'

I blush and he smiles.

'Thought so.'

'Do you mind?' I ask, hating myself for sounding so unsure of myself but terrified of his reaction. He looks happy.

'Of course not. I want to be your first.'

My stomach fizzes at the thought but the unwanted thought pops into my mind *Is that all he's after?* before he quells it, stroking my face and kissing me again.

'I don't want to rush you though; I want it to be right. I've never been anyone's first before. And besides' —he grins— 'we've only just got together. Trying to take advantage of me aren't you?'

He squeezes my butt and I laugh, feeling girlish and giddy and dying to tell Dannii, who will probably never believe that he isn't trying to get me drunk and drag me upstairs. That he's different.

And I'm thrilled that he's never been anyone's first, even though it makes me think it also means he's never been with anyone so inexperienced and wonder why he's so happy about it. What if I'm no good?

And then I realise something else. I'm taking it for granted that at some point, it's going to happen. I don't know exactly when over the last few days I decided I wanted to have sex with Joe, but I do know that yes, Joe is the one. Finally, I've met someone I'm ready to give my virginity up to.

And I'm totally terrified.

Chapter Five

After another glass of wine I feel more than tipsy, more like nauseous and tired, and Joe insists on walking me back.

'Can I stay at yours?' I ask, then instantly blush, realising what it sounds like. 'Not for…that. But I don't want Mum to know I've been drinking.'

Joe agrees, holding my coat out for me.

''Course you can, Steph won't mind, and I don't want your mum to get a bad impression of me before we've even met.'

I don't answer that, because the truth is I'm more concerned about Mum meeting Joe than I am about her knowing I've been drinking. She would probably be relieved to know I'm acting like a typical teenager and having a drink at a party, but I'm still not sure what her reaction to Joe will be. Fresh out of jail and living on the Estate? He's hardly every mother's dream, even though I feel disloyal for thinking it. I need to talk to her about him first, tell her what a good guy he really is, but I don't seem to be getting the chance lately, what with her newfound social life. I text her to say I'm staying at Dannii's and swiftly receive an *OK, don't be late for school. Love you.*

I feel guilty for lying. She trusts me.

When we get back to Joe's I'm nearly asleep on my feet and he steers me up to bed then goes to make me a coffee. I kick off my shoes and sit on the end of his bed. What do I do now? Even in my half-asleep half-drunken state I'm aware of the awkwardness of the situation. If I sleep in my clothes I'll have to walk home all smelly and rumpled in the morning but if I take them off it will look like an invitation. In the end I settle for removing my cardi and jeans, leaving me in a bra, vest and quite respectable boy shorts that cover my butt, then dive under the covers, pulling them up around me. I'm asleep before Joe even comes back up the stairs.

I wake up feeling disorientated. My mouth tastes foul, and for a moment I don't know where I am, then it comes back to me in a flash. I'm with Joe. In his bed.

His arm is draped over me and he's curled around me so that my butt is tucked into his groin. He stirs and I can feel him hard against me through our underwear. I've heard this is normal for lads in the morning, but even so I freeze, a tremble going through me that could be excitement or fear, or perhaps both. I don't move away though, enjoying the feel of him wrapped around me. His body is warm and firm, similar and yet so different from mine.

I feel his hand stroking my thigh. I stay still, eyes closed, not sure what to do. The world has dwindled to his hand on my skin, his breath on my neck and his obvious arousal pushed against the softness of my butt. I'm so turned on I want to turn around and jump on him, but I hold back. Not least because judging by the taste in my mouth I must have the worst death breath ever.

Joe kisses the back of my neck, little butterfly kisses that make me quiver. I squirm against him, giggling.

'Morning, sexy.'

He sounds far too bright and cheerful. I'm not great in the mornings.

'What time is it?'

'About seven, I reckon. My alarm hasn't gone off yet. I have to be at work at eight.'

'Urgh,' I moan, pulling the covers over my head. The cold reality of the early morning and my impending hangover cut through my arousal.

'I haven't got class 'til eleven. It's so early,' I whine. Joe chuckles, his voice extra deep and sexy with the added sleepiness.

'Stay here if you want. Steph won't mind; she makes a mean breakfast too.'

It sounds tempting, but what will she think? She'll assume we've had sex, and the thought of facing her over the breakfast bar while she bombards me with questions about what I'm getting up to with her nephew fills me with dread. I bury my face in the pillow.

The sound of Joe's alarm is shrill in the room, making me jump. Joe stretches lazily before getting out of bed. I peek under my pillow at him, at that lush body in his boxers, and a very obvious erection stretching them to a triangle in front of his body. I can't help giggling.

'You've got morning glory.'

Joe snorts.

'I've had it all night, Ash. Sleeping next to you all night and not touching you wasn't easy. You've got a lovely ass by the way.'

'You looked?'

He grins.

'I had a little peek when I got into bed. You were dead to the world. Snoring, in fact.'

'I was not!' I squeal, indignant. No one has ever told me I snore before. Then I think about the fact he was turned on all night lying next to me.

'You must have great self-control. Compared to other boys I mean.' Great, now I sound like sleeping next to boys in my underwear is a regular pastime for me.

Joe shrugs.

'I was locked up for six months. I can wait.'

'It must have been horrible. Jail I mean.' I pause, wondering if he'll get that closed off look he does when I mention his past, but he seems more open with me this morning. Something's changed between us, shifted.

'It wasn't too bad. Boring, mostly. I read a lot and used the gym, kept myself to myself. I'm not intending on going back there, I know that much.'

'Your aunt said you shouldn't have been there at all,' I probe. He sits down on the edge of the bed, close to me, putting his hand on my leg through the covers.

'I went too far, Ash. I saw this poor boy being picked on and it just made me mad. I kept hitting the guy who was bullying him when a warning probably would have done it, and I didn't care that people were watching. I hate bullies, but I acted like one really. Juvy made me think. I saw so many lads like me who had shitty backgrounds or whatever and you could tell the ones that would overcome it and the ones that would be thugs all their lives.'He glances up at the picture on the wall. 'I want Mum to be proud of me.'

He looks so vulnerable it makes my breath catch in my throat and I sit up and stroke his shoulder, forgetting about my death breath and bad hair. He sits up and gives a little shake as if literally pulling himself together, then turns and flashes me that wicked grin again.

'I need a shower. Want to join me?'

I feel myself go hot, flustered at the change of subject and the naughty suggestion, and open and close my mouth, not sure what to say. Joe ruffles my hair.

'I'm joking, go back to sleep.' And he disappears off for a shower. I lie back down, but there's no chance of going back to sleep now. I hear the hum of the water and imagine him standing there, naked, the water running down his body and slicking his hair to his head, and wish I was actually brave enough to just get up and get in there with him.

Breakfast is delicious but awkward. Steph doesn't ask me

anything personal but keeps giving me knowing looks until I want to just burst out 'I'm not having sex with him' but of course I don't. I'm too aware that there should be a 'yet' on the end of that statement too.

I need to talk to someone about this. There's so much I don't know. Dannii is the obvious choice of course, but for some reason I don't want to share this with her. I know sex doesn't mean much to Dannii, whereas my decision to sleep with Joe is massive, and she just won't get it. I don't want it reduced to a giggly conversation about the size of his willy or what position to do it in.

So after leaving Steph I end up at Rianne's. If anyone knows about consequences and bad decisions, it's her.

She opens the door looking as harassed as ever. Her hair's a mess and she looks as though she's lost weight in the last week. Her face lights up when she sees me though.

'Ash! Come in, I'm so bored. Gabe's sleeping a bit better, thank God, but if I have to watch anymore daytime talk shows I'm going to go crazy. I was just folding laundry.'

'Sounds fun.'

I help Rianne fold clothes while she chatters away about the baby and Mitch, who's back on day shifts and back at home. It sounds as though they're getting on better.

'So, enough about me. Any gossip?'

I can't help myself smiling, a proper split your face grin, as I tell her about Joe rescuing me in the park, and our date and our kisses and my decision that at some point, I want him to be my first. Rianne widens her eyes in excitement.

'Oh, wow, that sounds so romantic. You should go for it, Ash. I'm so jealous. My first time was with Mitch round the back of McDonalds after a bottle of cider. Not very classy.'

She looks sad for a minute.

'But you're still together, and you love him right?'

She nods enthusiastically.

'Oh, yeah, he's a good guy and a great dad. But it could easily have been so different. He could have been a total loser and not wanted to know, and I could never have done this on my own. I still wish I'd waited to get to know him too, so it was special. Imagine having to tell Gabe when he's older where he was conceived! We'll have to make something up.'

'You should call him Mac,' I quip, making her laugh before I say more seriously, 'That's what I wanted to talk to you about. You know, contraception and stuff.'

Rianne stops folding and stares at me, then bursts into near hysterical giggles. I frown, totally confused until she says, wiping away tears of laughter;

'Ash, you're hilarious. You want sensible advice on contraception so you ask someone who got pregnant at fifteen?'

She has got a point. I start laughing myself, realising the ridiculousness of the situation. After the laundry though we sit down with cans of Coke and crisp sandwiches – all Rianne gets time to eat, by the look of her – and we get serious again.

'You must use something now,' I point out.

'Oh, yeah. I love Gabe to bits but I couldn't do it again, it's so hard. As soon as we started talking about having sex again I went straight on the Pill. They do new ones now that are less dangerous for younger women and stuff.'

Maybe I need to book a doctor's appointment. But it just seems so grown up and, well, unsexy.

'You could just use a condom,' Rianne points out. I wince, remembering the time we had sex education class in the last year at school and had to practice putting condoms on these white cylinder things. I managed to rip a big hole in mine, whereas Dannii had the class in stitches and the teacher up in arms by demonstrating how to put one on with your mouth. Rianne missed that class; she had just found out she was pregnant.

Perhaps I should have gone to Dannii for advice after all. She's been on the Pill since the age of thirteen; that trip to the doctors was the extent of her mum's attempt to talk to her about the birds and the bees.

Being around mounds of baby clothes and looking at the bags under Rianne's eyes is probably all the advice I need, I muse as I phone the doctors on my way to sixth form to make an appointment for the morning. I freeze when the receptionist asks me the nature of my problem.

'Er, I need contraception,' I blurt out, glad she can't see my face. There's a pause. I can practically smell her disapproval.

'If it's emergency contraception you need, you can visit the GU clinic in the town centre and sit and wait. The sooner you take it after intercourse the more effective it is.' She says the whole thing in a monotone as if she's reading off a sheet of paper and it takes me a minute to realise what she means.

'Oh, no,' I protest. 'I haven't had sex yet.'

There's another pause, during which I shrivel up and die of embarrassment.

'I can get you in with Dr Cooke on Monday at ten forty,' she says and I'm sure there's now a little more warmth in her voice. Of course, I could just be imagining it.

'Lovely, thank you,' I say weakly. If I'm going to be this pathetic just talking to the receptionist, then seeing the doctor is going to be a nightmare.

When I get home from college later there's another nightmare waiting that drives all thoughts of the doctor out of my mind. As I hang up my jacket I can see Mum at the kitchen table. It's laid for dinner, and she's wearing a low cut lilac top that I haven't seen before, and her hair is all straightened out. She looks like Nicole Kidman.

'Look who's here for dinner.' She smiles at me, nodding her head towards the other edge of the table, which I can't see from where I'm standing. Even before I enter the kitchen, I know who it is.

'Hey, Princess.' Dad smiles at me, our phone conversation last night obviously forgotten. My stomach sinks. Is this where they tell me their happy news? I glare at him and then her in turn. Mum wrinkles her nose, puzzled.

'Your dad said he had arranged to see you tonight, so I thought it would be nice if we all had dinner together.'

'Great idea.' I chuck my bag onto the side and sit at the table. Mum starts doling dinner out. She's made moussaka, which always used to be Dad's favourite.

'You always were a good cook, Keira,' he says in a syrupy voice that makes me want to puke. I know I'm acting like I'm twelve again, but I don't care.

'Really? Is that why you left her for Anya?' Two pairs of horrified eyes swivel round at me.

'Ashley!' Mum gasps.

'It's okay, I guess I deserved that,' Dad says. I stand up, pushing my plate away.

'Do you know what, I'm not hungry, and I've got a stack of homework to do. Sorry.'

Dad calls after me as I'm going upstairs;

'I'll pick you up tomorrow then, Princess?'

'Sure.'

I catch a glimpse of Mum's face as I go up the stairs and she almost looks like she's going to burst into tears. Instantly I feel like a total bitch, but there's no way I'm going back to play happy families. I was hoping to talk to Mum tonight, maybe tell her about Joe and my decision, even ask her to come to the doctors with me, but there's no chance of that now. Not just because she'll be mad at me for being rude either. If I try and have a heart to heart with her I know she's going to tell me about her and Dad, and I just don't want to hear it.

As I sit upstairs with my homework unopened in front of me I can hear them talking, but although I strain to hear what they're saying their voices are too low. Mum sounds almost angry. Good, maybe she'll have second thoughts. After half an hour or so I hear her saying bye to him at the front door. There's a pause before he answers her. They're probably kissing.

Mum comes up and pops her head round the door, her big eyes full of concern rather than anger.

'Are you okay?'

'Yeah.'

'Can we talk?'

Oh God, here it comes.

'I'm busy,' I snap, seeing the hurt flash in her eyes before she gives up and goes, closing the door softly.

I sit fuming for a few more minutes before pushing my books to one side and turning on the computer. I check my Facebook, feeling pleased when I see Joe hasn't been online. I notice Dannii has changed her relationship status to 'single' and call her, parental problems momentarily forgotten.

'Have you and Dean split up?'

I can't say I'm surprised. Dannii's boyfriends rarely last long. Still, she seemed quite fond of him.

'Yeah, he's an idiot. He was supposed to pick me up today, then he went to the pub instead.'

'Doesn't sound that bad.'

'He was with his ex.'

That is bad. Not least because it means there's at least one other girl out there who was stupid enough to go out with him.

'Do you want me to come round?' I ask. I was hoping I would end up seeing Joe, but Dannii's my best friend, and that has to come before boys. Even if she has been getting on my nerves lately.

So I end up at Dannii's listening to her moan about Dean, which means I can't really get all gooey about Joe and have to sneak to the toilet to text him because I don't want to rub it in that I'm happy and she's not. Eventually though, she asks about him.

'So did you do the deed last night?'

'No, but I think it's on the cards.'

Instead of squealing with delight and bombarding me with sex advice like I expected Dannii to do she screws her face up.

'Are you sure you want to do this? I mean, he's not the type to stick around.'

I shake my head.

'He's not like that. I know everyone thinks he's a bad boy but he's not. I spent all last night with him and he didn't even lay a hand on me.'

Why is she so hostile? I know she worries about me, but it seems more than that. I wonder if she was warning him off me last night when they both disappeared.

'Well, it's up to you,' she shrugs and is about to say something else when her Blackberry beeps. She looks at it and gasps dramatically.

'Who is it?'

'Dean. Says I'm a stuck-up cow.' She starts jabbing at buttons like a typist on speed before pressing send with a flourish, looking pleased with herself.

'What did you put?'

'I told him he was a shit shag.' She grins, and I grin back, but inside I'm thinking *I hope me and Joe don't end up like this.*

But don't all relationships, sooner or later, end up like this? Look at my mum and dad, all those years together, working hard, raising a family and then poof, all gone. Dad runs off with some airheaded blonde who can barely speak a word of English and we're left to pick up the pieces. She was so strong, my mum, there was no crying or ranting in front of me or lying around in bed all day; in fact it was me that did all that, but for so long her smile didn't reach her eyes. Has she really forgotten all that, or is she so in love with him she can just forgive the last five years as if they never happened? Maybe it's not so surprising that up to now, all my love affairs have been inside my own head. Because now I've given Joe that power to hurt me, and I know I would never be flippant like Dannii if we broke up.

I am screwed up. We've only just got together and I'm worried about breaking up. I tell Dannii my thoughts and she leans over and hugs me, taking me by surprise.

'That's just parents for you babe. They mess us up.'

We snuggle up on the sofa and watch MTV for a bit, and I remember why in spite of all our differences we're still best friends.

I'm still thinking about her parent comment next day when Dad picks me up. He takes me for a meal, not a Big Mac or even a Frankie and Bennys's burger but a proper dinner in a posh restaurant on the outskirts of town.

'This is nice,' I say, looking around at the sparkling glasses and fancy décor, and the glamorous waitresses who all look like models.

'I used to bring your mum here. Of course, it was under different management then and a little more homely. Still, I used to have to save up all week to bring her here.'

I can't help smiling at this bit of nostalgia, even though I know exactly what he's doing. Taking a deep breath, I decide to take the bull by the horns.

'You still love her, don't you?'

He looks taken aback, then puts down his glass very carefully before clasping his hands on the table and looking straight at me. He's doing the 'we need to talk' face he did when he told me he was moving out because 'me and your mum think it's for the best'.

'I've never stopped loving her. I know how much I hurt you both, and believe me, so many times over the years I've wished I could turn the clock back.'

'But you can't,' I state the obvious.

'No, but I can do my best to make sure things are different in the future. I want to be here for you both.'

I don't know what to say to that, and I'm relieved when the waiter comes over with our food. I busy myself making a big show of cutting up my steak, even though it's such good quality the knife slides through it like butter. He really is pulling out all the stops; they probably cooked it up between them, Mum wisely staying out of the way after last night's cosy family dinner fiasco. I know he's trying and I appreciate it, but this is all because he wants to smooth the way to get back with Mum now Anya's dumped him, it's not about me, the daughter he so easily walked out on after a childhood of adoring him. I gulp at my drink as if I can wash down the bitterness that's bubbling up in me.

He must sense my thoughts because he stops chewing for a moment and gives me that sincere look again.

'I do really miss you, Princess. I'm so proud of how well you're doing.'

'I've got a boyfriend,' I blurt. He stares at me for a second, a range of emotions on his face, before putting on a bland expression and going back to his crab salad.

'Last week you said there was no one special.'

I shrug.

'There is now. I haven't told Mum yet.'

He raises an eyebrow at me.

'Don't you think you should?'

I nod, wishing now that I hadn't said anything. If I'm worried about Mum's reaction to Joe, his will no doubt be ten times worse. Things were so much easier when he was abroad.

'I'm going to. But she's been a bit *distracted* lately.'

He winces at my tone, the barb obviously hitting home. Good. We eat in silence for a while, before he starts asking questions, like I knew he would. At least he's not going gooey about Mum anymore.

'So how did you meet him, what does he do? How old is he?'

'Through Dannii, and he's a mechanic, at college too, he wants his own business one day, and he's eighteen.'

Well, it's all true. I've just left out the criminal record part. Dad nods as if satisfied.

'He sounds very nice. I'm assuming we will get to meet him soon?'

Now my parents are a 'we' again. How nice.

'Soon, yeah. I want to tell Mum myself first.'

He looks pleased, winking at me as if now we share some big secret.

'Okay, Princess, I'll keep it between us for now.'

This comrade thing makes me cringe. I don't believe him either; he'll go rushing back to Mum to tell her, so they can discuss how 'we' are going to support me in this. I give it a few days before there will be another attempt at a family dinner, this time with Joe invited. I wonder how he will feel if I ask him not to mention his past. I don't want him to think I'm ashamed of him, but neither do I want them judging him before they've gotten to know him. Like I so nearly did.

Thinking about Joe I glance at the ornate clock in the corner. I've arranged to meet him at the garage at four, which I'm looking forward to; it gives me a chance to see yet another side of him. I haven't mentioned my Monday morning appointment to him yet.

I get Dad to drop me a few streets away, and even though I can tell he's itching to get a look at Joe he agrees, ruffling my hair as I get out of the car. I've just spent ten minutes fixing it in the mirror.

I feel nervous as I follow the directions Joe gave me and approach the garage. I spot two guys outside in overalls having a fag and one of them whistles as I approach, the other looking me up and down appreciatively. I want to turn and bolt when Joe appears behind them looking unbearably sexy in his work trousers and a tight t-shirt covered in oil. He grins as he sees me, wiping his hands on a cloth before punching the guy that whistled playfully in the shoulder.

'Leave off boys; this one's mine.'

I feel weirdly flattered at his crude comment, especially when his friend turns and high fives him, then nods me a smiley hello. I smile shyly back, but my eyes are on Joe. I haven't seen him since he left early for work yesterday morning, and it's as if the sun has come out. He comes over and kisses me and I forget about parents, doctors and essays and pretty much everything apart from the nearness of him. He pulls back to look at me and his eyes are dancing. We beam at each other simultaneously.

'Come in,' he says. 'I've got to lock up, then we can head off.'

He leads me into the workshop, raising his hand in goodbye at his two workmates outside, who finish their cigarettes and slope off. I wrinkle my nose at the strong smell of metal and oil. It's pungent, but very manly somehow. I follow him into the 'office' which consists of a wooden table with invoices and car magazines all over it, an ancient laptop and a kettle and a few stained cups. As he's hanging up keys and shuffling bits of paper around I look at the laptop, which is already turned off.

'Been on Facebook today?'

My tone comes out accusatory rather than the nonchalance I was aiming for, but if he notices he doesn't mention it.

'Nah, it's been non-stop today, and Bill's off so he left me in charge.' He says the last bit proudly, and I feel pleased for him.

'He must think highly of you to leave you in charge of everything. I mean, you're only eighteen.'

'And a criminal? It's okay, Ash you can say it,' he says lightly, but his eyes look guarded. I shake my head.

'I wasn't even thinking that,' I say truthfully, and he comes over and kisses me.

'Sorry, I'm just being touchy. I still can't believe my luck; I was so proud when I saw you walking up and those idiots were looking at you with their tongues hanging out. You really don't know how pretty you are.'

I duck my head, embarrassed.

'Dannii's always been the pretty one,' I say, and he rolls his eyes.

'Dannii looks like every other girl trying too hard,' he says and I feel pleased, even if slightly disloyal. So I was wrong about him fancying her. Even so a look passes across his face that I can't quite read and he changes the subject.

'How were things with your dad?'

'Okay. He was trying to hint about getting back with my mum.'

Joe strokes a curl away from my face.

'Maybe he just wants to make amends. You're lucky; I haven't seen my dad since I was five.'

'That's awful. Did he just up and leave?'

I try to imagine Joe as a small boy, crying for his dad, and my heart hurts for him. Joe laughs, but it's a bitter sound rather than an amused one.

'Sort of. He's in prison for armed robbery. Mum never got over it.'

He looks angry, and I'm starting to understand why he's so tetchy about having been to prison.

'You're not like him you know,' I say on impulse, and snuggle into his chest He wraps his arm round me and I lean up on tiptoe to kiss him.

What starts as a tender moment quickly turns into a full on passionate kiss, with my butt pressed up against the edge of the table and his hand coiled in my hair, tugging on the back of my head gently. I explore his mouth with my tongue, the warm taste of him and the feel of his arms round me and the smell of oil and aftershave and sweat all combining to make my head spin. I'm lost. I'm so caught up in sensation that I scoot back on the table slightly and open my legs to pull him in between them, my feet hooking around the back of his calves. We're pressed together so tightly I can feel the heat of his body through his trousers and my jeans. I want to take his clothes off. I want him to take my clothes off. I arch into him, giving an involuntary whimper when his hand slips up my top and runs lightly over my bra. I don't freeze or try to stop him this time; I want him to touch me. He cups one breast in his hand and rolls my nipple gently between his fingers. I gasp at the sudden intense pleasure of it and kiss him harder, my tongue diving into his mouth. When he pulls away I think he's going to stop and disappointment zings through me until I realise he's lowering his head to my chest. He nips lightly at my nipple where it peeks between my bra and my top and for a second I freeze, torn between how good it feels and the realisation that I've never been this far with a boy. It feels so unbearably intimate that I want to both pull away and push myself further into his mouth all at the same time. His hand is in between my legs, pressing through my jeans, massaging in small insistent circles. I feel almost dizzy, an urgent feeling growing in my belly that I can't put a name to, but I know I don't want him to stop. Yet when his hand goes to my zipper I push it away without thinking and he straightens up, his breath coming in pants.

'Sorry, I got carried away,' he gasps, resting his chin against my forehead. I rearrange my top and bra, too shy to meet his eyes. Not just because of what we've just done, but also because part of me wishes I hadn't moved his hand away. Me, the good girl, the virgin, wanting to do it right here and now on a messy table in a grubby office. I'm not sure if I feel embarrassed or liberated. I bury my face in his chest to hide my conflicting emotions and he strokes my hair as if petting a kitten. My own breath is just as shaky as his.

'You turn me on so much,' he whispers in my ear. I love that, love that I can hear in his voice and feel in his body how much he wants me. It makes me feel sexy and grown up and aware of my own body in ways I've only read about before.

Even so, I'm aware of how soon all this is, even though it feels like I've known him for ages and can't imagine how there ever was a life before Joe. It seems crazy that it was just over a week ago I met him at Dannii's and thought how rude he was. How he so wasn't my type.

The thought that the way he is with me now could all be an act, that as Dannii prophesised he'll be gone as soon as he gets what he wants, chills me and I pull away, wrapping my arms around myself. He looks down in surprise at my sudden withdrawal.

'Are you okay? I didn't mean to do anything you didn't want me to.'

'I do want you to, that's the problem,' I blurt out. He looks at me in bemusement.

'I want to. Go further, I mean. But I don't want it to be…' I wave my hand, unable to put my feelings into words, not wanting to seem needy. But he seems to know exactly what I mean, grabbing my hand and pressing my fingertips to his lips.

'I want it to be special too,' he murmurs, his eyes gazing so intensely into mine that I have to look away. 'Why do you think I'm trying so hard to hold off? Normally I'd…' he trails off, and I flinch at his words, aware he was about to mention his past experiences. Or one of them. I swallow as I ask a question that's been on my mind for the past two days, needing to know even though I don't want to.

'Have there been many?'

He frowns for a moment before he realises what I mean.

'Girls? Not really. I've had two relationships, and there were a couple of girls at parties…only one since I got out.'

I feel my face fall at that. I had assumed there had been no one since prison, but why wouldn't there have been? He's gorgeous, mature, cool. Everything I'm not. He peers at me, still frowning.

'It doesn't matter does it?'

He looks so worried and strangely vulnerable that I can't help smiling.

'No, of course not.'

Okay, I'm lying, I'm insanely jealous at the thought of him so much as kissing anyone else, but I know I need to get a grip. He's eighteen, of course he's had relationships.

'You don't think it's weird?' I ask, 'that I've never really had a boyfriend?' I cringe as I say it. Joe looks thoughtful.

'Not weird,' he says slowly, choosing his words, 'but I wouldn't have expected it. You're pretty, and smart, and I can't understand why you wouldn't have all the boys chasing you. So I was a bit surprised.'

'You don't think I'm a prude?'

Joe snorts with laughter and I have to laugh with him. After all, we were just getting all hot and steamy in his boss's office.

'I think it's a good thing,' he says seriously. 'Too many girls just give it up, you know? I know that's a bit hypocritical, because I'm a guy and I've had one-nighters, but it's nice to meet a girl who's got respect for herself.'

I roll my eyes at that. Typical boy opinion. But even so I'm pleased that's what he thinks about me.

'I really, really want you,' he says seriously now, 'but I want it to be the right time. And place.'

He motions at the desk and I laugh, feeling any tension drain from my body. I jump down off the table, steadying myself on his arm.

'Let's get out of here,' he murmurs and I follow him out of the garage as he does his last minute checks and then locks up. I link my arm through his as we walk to the bus stop, feeling relaxed and happy, my worries forgotten.

For the moment at least.

Chapter Six

Monday morning arrives and I remember my appointment at the doctors. I talk Dannii into coming with me, even though I know she has English on Monday mornings.

'I'll get behind,' she protests grumpily when I knock on her door and explain where I'm going.

'You're already behind,' I point out, 'because you never want to get out of bed. If you come with me, I'll do your assignment for you.'

That does the trick, and we're soon sitting in the reception at our local surgery, which is painted a sickly green and smells of cough sweets. Dannii sits flicking through a magazine while I clock watch. Although I'm twenty minutes early, I don't get in to see the doctor until forty minutes after my appointment time. I leave Dannii in reception, now furiously texting Dean who 'won't leave me alone, the idiot' though she seems to be sending more texts than she's receiving.

I feel more than a bit nervous as I go into the doctor's room. It's a GP I haven't seen before, but thankfully a woman, though she is in her sixties and rather stern looking, with little glasses and an iron-grey bob hair sprayed to within an inch of its life. She waves me into the chair next to her without looking up.

'What's the problem, Miss Evans?' she asks, looking at my notes on the screen in front of her and sounding bored. For a minute I'm tempted to make something up about a sore throat and avoid the whole subject but I steel myself, reminding myself that I'm being grown up and sensible and have no reason to be embarrassed at all. After all, how can I think I'm ready to have sex if I can't even bring myself to talk about it?

'I wanted to ask about contraception,' I say, staring at the floor as she finally looks up.

'You're seventeen aren't you?' she says suspiciously, peering at my details on the screen and then nodding to herself. 'Have you had intercourse yet?'

'Er, no.'

She looks at me fully and gives me an approving smile, which makes me feel a lot less embarrassed.

'Well, good for you for coming to me first. Have you thought about which style of contraception would suit you?'

'The Pill?' I say, wondering just how many 'styles' there are. I've had the sex education classes, of course, but the only contraception advice I can remember is the previously mentioned condom on the fake willy incident, which was enough to put a girl off for life.

The doctor then hands me a leaflet, opening it to a chart in the middle listing various types of contraception and their pros and cons, she then proceeds to tell me about them all in detail until my mind boggles, making me feel slightly queasy when she describes graphically how a coil is inserted. I'm on the verge of bolting and telling Joe I don't want to have sex ever when she finally stops talking and beams at me.

'So, yes, I think one of the newer, lower hormone pills will be best for a girl your age.'

I nod enthusiastically, ready to take my prescription and go, but she hasn't finished with me yet. She takes my blood pressure and my height and weight, then just as I'm about to escape she asks, 'I'm assuming your prospective partner is a virgin too?'

I shake my head and she purses her lips at me, less impressed now.

'Then you really need to use condoms unless he has had

a recent sexual health check.'

Then she gives me dire warnings about STIs and the recent rise in Chlamydia among young people until I feel queasy again. Finally I emerge back into reception clutching my prescription and a small paper bag containing a selection of condoms and I'm mortified to discover as I'm walking out the door with Dannii, a selection of flavoured lubricants.

'Oooh, look,' she says in excitement pulling out a small brightly coloured sachet, 'you've got one that makes your bits tingle.'

'Put it away,' I hiss, grabbing it back off her and putting the lot into my handbag. We go into the nearby chemist to get my prescription and I'm half expecting the chemist to say something or give me a look of disgust, but she passes me my order without even looking up.

As we sit on the bus I read the instructions inside the packet, grimacing as I read the list of possible side effects.

'It says here it can make you gain weight and get acne,' I grumble. 'Sounds great. No wonder its effective, it makes you so ugly no one wants to have sex with you.'

Dannii snorts with laughter before pointing out, truthfully even if somewhat arrogantly, 'I'm on it and I have perfect skin and a great figure.'

I nod, conceding her point although I have to smile at her totally unselfconscious assessment of herself. It must be amazing to be so secure about the way you look, I think with a touch of jealousy. But then I remember that I have a boyfriend and parents who at least try to do a good job, and think that perhaps looks aren't everything.

All day long I'm all too aware of the bag of condoms in my handbag and can't wait to go home and get rid of them. After the doctor's lecture on sexually transmitted diseases just thinking about them makes me feel a bit icky. I feel ridiculously naive for not even thinking of that. I can't help remembering Joe's words 'there have been a few girls at parties' and wondering if it's possible he's carrying something. I've gone from feeling all grown up and womanly to like an inexperienced child again, and cringe at the thought of asking him. I don't want him to take offence. When I get home I put my Pill packets in my make-up bag so they're in an easy place for me to remember to take them every morning but stash the bag of condoms and lubricants in the bottom of my wardrobe. As an afterthought I take out one of the condoms and put it in my handbag. I feel a bit guilty for hiding them, especially because I've always assumed I would be tackling these issues with Mum's advice. I know she'll be hurt when she finds out I haven't confided in her, and I feel a pang of hurt at the strange gulf that's opened up between us recently. Because of Dad, I think angrily, slamming the wardrobe door shut.

I can hardly meet her eyes during dinner, and tell her I'm going round a classmates to study when I'm really going to see Joe. He meets me at the park as always, refusing to let me walk through there or the Estate on my own, mostly because of Jason and his crew I think. When we reach his house Steph greets me warmly, winking at me as we head up the stairs. I think of the condom in my bag and blush as I follow Joe into his room. Now is the time to talk about it with him, I know, but the thought of having the conversation makes me want to bolt, just like I wanted to at the doctors but even more strongly. I'm worried he'll think I'm too forward, going and putting myself on the Pill before I've even talked about it with him. Before we've even had sex and we've only been going out for just over a week. Or maybe he'll take it as an indication that I'm ready now, and I'm not sure that I am.

I take a deep breath, psyching myself up, while Joe looks

at me with a worried expression on his face.

'Aren't you going to sit down?'

'I need to tell you something.'

A shadow crosses his face and he folds him arms, his face taking on the sullen expression he had when I met him. I falter, unsure how to continue. He's virtually glaring at me now.

'Well, go on then, spit it out.' His tone makes me wince.

'I talked to the doctor about going on the Pill today, and I was just wondering' —my words come out in such a rush they're tripping over each other— 'if we need to use anything else when, if, we have sex, because you, er, said you'd been with a few girls.' The last bit comes out as one long exhale and I gasp with relief as I finish, peering at him anxiously. He takes me by surprise as he closes the distance between us and pulls me into a hug. He feels like he's trembling and as I look up I see he's struggling not to laugh.

'How is this funny?' I demand in outrage. Joe just shakes his head, grinning down at me.

'Well?'

'It's not that what you said is funny, it's just that when you said you had to tell me something...'

'Yes?' I snap at him, completely confused. He stops grinning and looks embarrassed.

'I thought you were going to tell me you didn't want to see me anymore.' He shuffles from one foot to the other, and I feel a rush of love for him. That's why he looked so pissed off, why he got that defensive expression. I touch his lips then place a light kiss on them, and he looks happy again.

'Why on earth would you think that,' I murmur, not really expecting an answer, which is just as well because he just shrugs, a gesture of his I'm starting to understand as 'I don't want to get into that conversation right now'.

'So, about the condom thing?' I prompt, feeling less embarrassed about the whole topic now we've established what it was I needed to say.

'I had a full medical in jail, and I used a condom with that girl after I got out. Does that answer your question? But I don't mind wearing one if you want me to.'

He would sound a lot more convincing if he hadn't said that with such a look of abject martyrdom on his face but still, I appreciate the sentiment. The whole 'that girl' thing bothers me too.

'Who was she?'

He looks surprised.

'Just some girl, Ash. I doubt that you'd know her. I've never seen her since.'

That makes me feel a bit better, but paradoxically I don't like the way he speaks about this unnamed girl. Surely sex should be more important than that?

'What's wrong?'

I look at him with what I hope is a stern expression, though I feel my eyes soften as I look at his face. He looks so boyish and cute when he's not scowling, it makes me melt.

'I don't want you to ever talk about me like that. You know, that I'm 'just some girl'.'

He pulls me towards him again and tugs at a curl near the side of my face.

'You're already a lot more than that to me. You must know that?'

His eyes search my face, looking unsure of himself again. I nod, snuggling against him, trying to ignore the small gnawing doubt that still remains. It's just my own insecurities, I tell myself.

Joe seems reluctant to really touch me for the rest of the

evening, and I can't tell if I've hurt his feelings or if he's trying to be careful around me so I don't think he's just after the one thing. We have a brief snog when he walks me back, me leaving earlier than expected.

'I do need to study,' I tell him, though really I just want to go home and think about things. He pulls back from me looking worried.

'We're okay aren't we?'

'Of course,' I reassure him, squeezing his hand, surprised at this more sensitive side of him.

'I really do care about you, Ash. More than care, I think.'

My heart does a backflip at his words. Is he trying to tell me he loves me, or thinks he might? I can't stop the smile from stretching my cheeks.

'Me too,' I say, and we both stand there grinning like idiots and holding hands before we finally tear ourselves away from each other and I practically skip the rest of the way home. I feel so happy, I decide I'm going to go home and tell Mum about Joe, and talk to her about whatever's going on with her and Dad. I've been horrible the past few days and I'm starting to feel guilty.

When I get in I can hear low music from Mum's room upstairs and smile to myself. Sometimes when she wants to relax she'll lie in her room with her music on and doodle in her scrapbooks or even read one of my romances. It'll be easier to talk to her if she's in a mellow mood. I'm surprised to find I'm even quite looking forward to it. I hang up my coat and go upstairs, noticing her door is half-open. I run up the last couple of steps.

And freeze.

Through the half-open door I can see her, half obscured but undoubtedly naked, her head tipped back, eyes closed and lips half parted, her glorious curls falling back over the bed. Rearing above her, his back to me, are the unmistakable dark curls of my dad.

'No!' I shout, thumping on the door in a rage before turning and running back down the stairs, hot tears hitting my cheeks and rolling down my face onto my chest.

'Ashley!' I hear Mum shriek behind me. 'Wait!' But I'm out the front door and running down the path before she's got time to get dressed and come after me. I hear Sabre bark behind me and pause just to shut the gate so he can't get out then I'm running again, my vision blurry with tears and the sound of my own heart beat angry and fierce in my ears. How could they? I ask myself over and over as I run. How could they? Okay, I was prepared for the possibility they might get back together but to see that…I feel sick and angry and for reasons I can't explain even betrayed. I carry on running until I get a cramp in my side and my chest feels ready to explode and then stop, leaning on my knees as I catch my breath. I'm at the park. Without even consciously thinking about it I've run towards Joe's. I hesitate, wondering if I should really go to him with this, and wary of walking through the park where I was harassed before, but I know there's no one else I want to run to, not even Dannii.

I walk through the park with my head down, my steps brisk, but thankfully it's empty anyway. I feel exhausted and drained by the time I get to Joe's house and seeing my reflection in the glass down the centre of the front door I can tell I look a total state. My hair's all over the place and my mascara is making dirty tracks down my cheeks where I've been crying. I rub furiously at my face as the door opens but it obviously doesn't help as Steph stares at me in horror.

'Jesus, child, you look like no one owns you,' she exclaims as she ushers me in, looking horrified. 'Whatever's the matter?'

'Is Joe in?' I snuffle, but before she can answer Joe is there, practically shoving Steph to one side and grabbing me by the arms, looking alarmed as I burst into tears again.

'What is it? Has someone hurt you? Tell me who it was.'

'No,' I say quickly, wiping at my eyes, 'nothing like that.'

As I explain what's happened through my sobs I start to feel a bit silly. Compared to the things Joe has been through it sounds so trivial, but I can't shake off the image of them together or sort through the mess of emotions it's churned up inside me. Steph makes a cup of tea that she pushes into my hand before making herself scarce and Joe follows me up to his room where I sit on the bed, shaking from the crying and running so far without a coat.

'I'm cold,' I say and Joe pulls his jumper off and drapes it round my shoulders. Even in this mess I feel a pulse of desire at the sight of his toned torso and the thick muscles in his arms.

'You might be in shock,' he says, sitting next to me and pulling me onto his lap. His skin is warm and comforting and I lay my head on his chest.

'I'm sorry,' I whisper.

'For what?'

'Coming to you with this, when you've been through so much with your own mum and dad. I must sound stupid.'

He kisses the top of my head.

'Don't be daft. I think you need to talk to them when you've calmed down, but not right now.'

I feel like I don't want to talk to either of them ever again.

'It was just gross,' I say, trying to blot out the image of my own mother with her head thrown back over the bed. Joe chuckles.

'It's always gross knowing your parents are at it. But

you have to remember as your mum's only young really, she's got to have a life of her own.'

'Did you ever catch yours?' I ask curiously. He shakes his head.

'I was small when Dad got sent down, and there was never anyone else for Mum. She was waiting for him to get out. He's only got a couple of years now, but then of course she got sick.' His voice sounds strangled and I sit up, pulling him to me now. The awful sadness of his story makes me want to cry all over again.

'Your poor dad,' I say, and Joe looks at me with disgust.

'Don't try and make it all romantic, Ash. If he hadn't got himself locked up she wouldn't have been on her own all those years and maybe she wouldn't have got sick.'

And you wouldn't have been left on your own, I think. I know he's got Steph and she's lovely, but it can't be the same. We sit in silence for a few moments, just holding each other, before he asks.

'What is it you're so worried about? That he'll come between you and your mum?'

I shake my head but even as I do I wonder if there's an element of that. After all it's been just the two of us for so long. But mostly, I'm just worried for her.

'I don't trust him,' I try to explain. 'I know that sounds awful because he's my dad but he walked out on her before, how can she believe he won't do it again?' It makes me mad that she could be that stupid, that she can just take him back as soon as he comes creeping with his tail between his legs.

Joe lies me back on the bed and spoons in behind me, his arms wrapped around me, making me feel safe. He doesn't talk, just holds me and I feel myself relax. It seems so right, lying with him like this, and after a while I drift off to sleep, leaving my tea to go cold on the dresser.

When I wake up it's dark and Joe's arms are heavy around me. I stretch my legs, stiff and groggy as I come to and take in where I am. The events of the evening come back to me and I feel a stab of anger towards my parents and then guilt at running off and not telling Mum where I am. Or at least lying and making out I'm at Dannii's. I left my phone in my coat pocket when I ran out and for a moment I panic, then decide if she was running around looking for me than either Dannii or Rianne would have directed her here. No doubt she's too busy with Dad and is probably glad to get rid of me, I can't help but think bitterly.

As I turn over, shifting Joe's arm where it lies heavy across my chest he murmurs and stirs, opening his eyes and looking at me. For a second he looks confused, then I see the sleep fog clear from his eyes and he smiles like he's pleased to see me. He sits up and stretches, the muscles in his shoulders tensing and rippling. I sit up and run my fingertips down his naked back and then back up. Feeling bold I drag my fingernails across his skin, scratching him oh so lightly. He makes a funny sound low in his throat and turns to me with an intense look on his face. He crushes his mouth against mine and I respond hungrily, as if he's food and I haven't eaten for days. The taste and smell and feel of him drives all thoughts and worries about earlier from my mind and I pull him down on top of me, breaking away from our kiss and nipping at his neck, then drawing his ear lobe into my mouth and sucking on it. His whole body gives a little shudder and he groans. His hands slide up my body and disappear under my shirt and I lift my back to allow him more room. His hands slide up my back and down again, around my stomach and up to my breasts and I arch up again, trying to let him know without words that yes, I want him. He pushes my top up my body and I wriggle out of it as he fumbles at my bra. It takes a few moments for him to unclip it, then he takes it off with a tenderness that almost makes me cry again. Topless before him, I have to fight the urge to cover my boobs with my hands.

Because he's staring at me as if I'm the most gorgeous thing he's ever seen, which is lovely but kind of embarrassing too. I feel so exposed I pull him down to kiss me, more to break the eye contact than out of passion, but it quickly turns passionate. His hands and then mouth are all over my boobs, and I can feel the heat growing in my body. I reach my hand down to the front of his jeans and unlike the first time in the car, he doesn't stop me. Feeling brave I go for his zipper.

I fumble to get my hand inside his boxers, then gasp as I come into contact with him. It feels thicker and harder than I had imagined and although the feel of him turns me on I'm nervous too. I just can't imagine how he will fit inside me.

I slide his jeans and boxer shorts over his hips and wrap my hand around him. He puts his hand over mine and moves it in long slow strokes and I can feel him pulse beneath my hand. His eyes are closed and his breath coming in gasps and I feel almost powerful. Then he moves my hand away, pinning it back behind my head and leaning down to kiss me again.

'You're so sexy,' he breathes into my mouth and I kiss him hard in response and grind my hips into him. He takes the hint and unzips my own jeans, pulling them slowly down my thighs and then kissing his way back up my body, little light touches that make me shiver. He strokes me through my knickers, gently then more insistently. There's a question in his eyes and in answer I lift my hips so he can slide them down. I close my eyes, feeling shy again as his gaze drinks me in. He looks at me like I'm beautiful, but it's an almost scary feeling. I've never been naked like this in front of a guy, and I can't imagine ever getting used to it. Still, when he touches me, his fingers stroking carefully between my thighs, I part my legs for him without even thinking about it. He slips a finger inside me and I gasp.

'Does it hurt?' he stops, looking concerned. I shake my head, opening my eyes and smiling at him.

'It doesn't hurt at all,' I whisper.

We touch each other for a while longer, exploring each other, and I soon forget my shyness, losing myself in each new sensation. I feel kind of awkward and fumbly, it's no Hollywood movie or even a scene from one of my romances, but somehow everything is just right. After a while we stop and he pulls himself up on his hands, leaning over me. He's lying in between my legs now and I can feel his erection nudging against me. I rub myself against it, trying to let him know I'm ready, but he looks unsure.

'Do you want to?' he asks, and I nod, biting my lip.

'You're sure? Because I don't want to rush you.'

'Sssh,' I say. 'I'm sure.'

Then I think of something.

'Have you got a condom?' I blush as I say it but he nods quickly.

'Yeah, hang on.' He gets up and goes to a drawer and I sit up, cold without the heat of his body on me and feeling exposed. I hope I haven't ruined the moment. But I left my bag when I ran out and I can't start taking those Pills until my next period. I don't want to have any regrets in the morning. I want it to be perfect, even though I know nothing is ever perfect and Dannii says the first time is always rubbish.

As he comes back over and kneels in front of me I panic, wondering if he'll expect me to put it on for him, but thankfully he does it himself, cursing when he realises it's inside out and has to start again. I giggle and feel more relaxed knowing he's not so smooth himself.

I feel myself tense when he lies me back and moves back to his position between my thighs but he doesn't go straight for it. Instead he kisses me and touches me with his hands again until I'm pulling at his hips wanting him, and only then does he start to nudge himself inside me.

There's a sudden intense pressure, not pain exactly, more a slight stretching sensation, then my body relaxes and as he begins to move in me it feels nice. Really nice. I lift my legs up and grab his bum, feeling his muscles tense as he moves. He looks down at me with that unreadable expression and his next words take me by surprise.

'I love you, Ash.'

I gasp and open my mouth to say it back but I'm cut off by him kissing me hard. I grip him tighter, overcome with emotion and I feel my body moving in time with his.

We're finally doing it. Me and Joe.

And it's perfect, it really is.

Over breakfast the next morning I have to pinch myself to make sure it's not all a dream. I keep staring at Joe, watching him wolf down the bacon and eggs Steph has made for us before going off to her cleaning job, watching the way the muscles in his jaw move as if transfixed. He catches me looking and beams at me, fork halfway to his mouth, and his egg slides off and plops onto the plate. He looks down and laughs.

'I'm like a love struck teenager,' he says, shaking his head.

'Er, you are a teenager,' I point out. He pulls a face at me, then chuckles again. I love the way his face creases up when he laughs.

'You make me feel happy,' he says simply, and goes back to his breakfast while I sit bubbling with joy. My stomach is too fluttery with butterflies to eat. It's not just the fact that we had sex, although it has in some undefinable way changed things between us, made it feel more real perhaps, it's the fact he said 'I love you'. I know it was in the heat of the moment, but it doesn't occur to me to doubt it. I just wish he had given me more of a chance to say it back. Announcing it over bacon doesn't feel appropriate somehow.

Instead I wait until we part company on the way to his work and sixth form, and blurt it out as we're kissing goodbye.

'I love you too you know,' I say, as if needing to reaffirm the fact that he said it first.

'I know,' he says airily, then adds before I can playfully thump him for being so arrogant, 'I've never felt like this about a girl.'

He goes off to work, not looking back, while I stand gobsmacked staring after him.

Classes speed by, with me barely aware of anything said to me and my face aching from smiling so much. When I get a call from Mum at lunch telling me to come straight home this afternoon because she wants to talk, even the memory of my discovery last night can't shake my good mood. After all, I reason to myself, if this is how Dad makes her feel, how can I begrudge her that? My blossoming love for Joe is casting a rosy glow over everything.

I feel like I've got a naughty secret too. As I shift around on the uncomfortable wooden chairs in History I feel a slight soreness in my body, not painful exactly but slightly raw, but I almost welcome the sensation as it brings with it a flashback of Joe inside me last night. Finally, I get what the fuss is all about.

It's as if there's a kind of aura around me, and I'm amazed no one else can see it. Like a neon sign flashing above my head that says 'I'm not a virgin anymore!'. But of course everyone goes about their usual day without noticing anything, apart from maybe the fact that I'm grinning like an idiot. To me, though, I feel changed, like my whole body has changed, and as if there should be some outward difference. I've had sex! And not just sex. Sex with Joe.

I almost skip home. Although I am worried about facing Mum, I'm confident we can talk and sort everything out. I can't stop her being with Dad, I can't stop them loving each other, any more than anything or anyone could stop me loving Joe. Today, the world feels like a better place.

Until, that is, I get home.

I assumed Mum wanted to talk to me about her and Dad, and I had decided in my loved-up state that I was going to be understanding and not act like a sulky teen, but as soon as I see the look on her face I know it's not going to go like that.

I'm in trouble.

I haven't seen that look on her face since I got caught playing truant, but I know exactly what it means; she's disappointed in me. And totally furious.

'Er, hi,' I say brightly, but she doesn't speak. She's just sitting at the kitchen table, regarding me with that look, which makes me feel about eight years old again. I wonder if she's mad at me for running off and not coming back all night, which would be pretty justified, but as I open my mouth to explain she holds up a hand to cut me off.

'Just sit down please.'

I pull out a chair opposite her, my eyes darting around the room until they come to rest on the object sitting on the table in front of her, and my heart sinks into my stomach like a lead weight. No butterflies now.

The bag of condoms from the doctor, with its colourful selection of lubricants in little plastic packets sits on the table like a time bomb.

Shit.

I don't know what to do or say so I go on the defensive, crossing my own arms in mimicry of her posture and glaring at the table.

'You've been snooping around my room,' I accuse. It's not just a tactic; I genuinely feel hurt. I've never known Mum to pry through my things, and now I wonder if she's always done it, if she's never trusted me as much as I've thought.

'Just as well,' she snaps, 'as you clearly weren't going to mention this to me yourself.'

I shrug, feeling guilty for not confiding in her and angry at her hypocrisy all at the same time. Although to be fair I suppose her affair with Dad has been kind of obvious, but I've been avoiding talking about it. Just as I've kept Joe from her. I shift uncomfortably as she taps her nails on the tabletop, waiting for some kind of explanation. All of a sudden I don't want to tell her anything, don't want my special moments with Joe to be viewed as if I've done something wrong.

'I've done nothing wrong,' I snap. 'I'm seventeen. I'm going to have sex sooner or later. I would have thought you would be happy I'm prepared.'

'You're more than prepared, Ashley,' she bites back, her eyes narrowed. I hardly recognise her like this, all cold and harsh. Part of me wants a hug, wants my loving smiley Mum, but then the image of her last night, rolling around with Dad, comes to me and I sneer, looking away with disdain. She carries on regardless, her words clipped and hard, hammering into the space between us like nails. 'And I found the Pill packets too. And one of these boxes has been opened and has a condom missing. What the hell is going on?'

'What do you think?' I retort. Mum sucks in an angry breath.

'Well, who is it? The boy you went on the date with?'

I shrug and then nod, kicking at the table leg. I know I'm not helping myself here, acting like a sulky kid when I could be using the opportunity to have the heart to heart I wanted, but I can't seem to help it.

'You've only known him for five minutes. You don't know anything about him!'

A sudden desire to lash out makes me answer her, telling her the things I've been hiding.

'What do you want to know? He lives on the Estate, and he's not long got out of jail. Juvenile offenders. His mum's dead and his dad's in prison for armed robbery. And yes, I'm having sex with him. Happy?'

Mum's mouth falls open in shock, but she regains her composure quickly, drawing herself up and taking a deep breath. I know that means she's angry, and trying to keep her temper in check, and for some reason that makes me mad and want to provoke her. Her next words tip me over the edge.

'How can you be so irresponsible?' She shakes her head as if she can't believe my stupidity.

That does it. I stand up in a fury, pushing the chair away.

'How am I irresponsible?' I shout indignantly. 'I'm seventeen! I went to the doctors and sorted contraception out first. How much more responsible do you want me to be? At least I'm not like you, having a baby at sixteen. You should be happy! You were always worrying about me not being interested in boys, and now I am and you're acting like this.'

I stop and take a breath, angry tears stinging my eyes. This is so unfair.

'That's the whole point,' she shouts back. 'You've always been so sensible, and now you're running around having sex with some boy you don't even know who sounds like a complete idiot.'

I bristle furiously at that, ignoring the little voice in the back of my brain that points out I did just deliberately paint the worst picture of him possible.

'At least he's not running around behind my back!' I scream, seeing the hurt flash in her eyes as I bring that up, again. 'And at least you didn't come in and catch me in bed like a bitch on heat.'

Mum jumps to her feet at that and for a horrible moment I think she's going to slap me, but instead she just hisses through her teeth at me.

'Get out of my sight'.

'Fine.' I stomp upstairs to my room like I really am eight years old again, slamming the door behind me. I sit there fuming, struggling not to cry. The day started off so well, I was so happy, but now I feel wretched. And as angry as I am at my mum, I can't believe I was so evil to her.

I'm debating with myself whether or not to go down and apologise when she knocks at my door and then pops her head round.

'Come in,' I say tearfully, relieved to see she looks calmer.

'I'm sorry I called you irresponsible,' she says softly. 'I was just hurt that you hadn't confided in me. But going to see the doctor was very sensible and I'm proud of you for that.'

I smile, wiping the tears that bubble over my lashes onto my sleeve. I'm about to say sorry back when she continues;

'But I don't think it's a good idea that you see this boy anymore.'

I gape at her.

'He sounds like bad news, Ashley, and I don't want you throwing yourself away on some criminal. I may have made mistakes, but at least me and your father stayed together and raised you and did our best to lead decent lives. How can you want to be with someone like that?'

'But, Mum,' I protest, realising just how much damage I've done with my comments about Joe, 'I was just trying to shock you. He's really nice, he works and he's lovely to me and…' I trail off as Mum raises her hand.

'Is it true? That he's been to prison?'

I nod dumbly.

'For what?'

'Fighting. Assault. But he was protecting someone. Mum honestly, if you meet him, you'll understand.'

She just shakes her head at me.

'If that's the case then why haven't I already met him or even been told about him?'

There's nothing I can say to that. I haven't told her about Joe because I was afraid this would be her reaction, and now I've gone and caused exactly what I was scared of. I try to protest again, but her mind's made up.

'I don't want you to see him anymore. You're grounded for the rest of the evening. I'll be having a word with your father later.'

The mention of Dad makes me mad again. If I hadn't caught them in bed together yesterday none of this would even have happened.

'You're a hypocrite,' I spit at her. 'You haven't told me what you've been getting up to have you? Do you think that's what I want?'

But she looks unmoved.

'I am an adult, Ashley, I don't need your approval. As for...my situation...we were both going to sit you down and talk to you about it this week. I wasn't expecting you back so early yesterday. I'm sorry you had to see that. But that doesn't change anything.'

'Go to hell,' I snap, furious. Grounded! I haven't been grounded since I was thirteen. It occurs to me that she can't stop me if I decide to get up and walk out, but then a feeling of being completely drained takes over me and I turn my back, curling up into a ball like I used to do in the days after Dad left.

'Ash...' I hear her take a step towards me, her voice full of concern now.

'Go away,' I say, and she does, closing the door quietly behind her. I sit like that for ages, crying silently to myself because I don't want her to hear, before I uncurl and lie down on the bed, wishing I was back in Joe's arms and none of this had happened.

How long I lie here I don't know, but when the door knocks again it's growing dim outside. I sit up, feeling heavy and drained. I can't cope with another argument.

'Come in.' Maybe she's calmed down, and I can explain to her about Joe. Or maybe it's Dad. Oh God, I so can't deal with this right now.

But it's neither of them. It's Dannii's pretty blonde head that pops round my door this time, and on seeing the state of me she rushes over and sits down next to me, shutting the door behind her.

'Oh my God, are you okay? I knew there was something wrong when I saw your Mum's face. Is it Joe? I bet he's dumped you hasn't he?'

'No of course not.'

Am I imagining things or is there a flicker of disappointment in her eyes?

'What's wrong then?'

I fill her in on what's happened with Mum without going into detail about me and Joe. Even so that's the first thing she picks up on.

'So you've done it then?'

I nod, unable to stop myself grinning in spite of my upset.

'Yeah, last night. It was really nice though Dannii, he was really gentle and—'

'Isn't it a bit soon?' she cuts in. I screw my face up in surprise. Huh? Coming from her?

'God you sound like Mum,' I complain, annoyed. 'Why can't you just be happy for me?'

'I'm just worried about you that's all. One minute you're hardly interested in boys at all, and now you're shagging some ASBO wannabe. I can understand what your Mum's saying, Ash.'

I can't believe this. Out of everyone, Dannii should understand. I think back to the last couple of weeks, to the way she's been about me and Joe and the way she drapes herself over him. 'You're jealous,' I say, realising as I say it that it's the truth. Dannii looks shocked, then laughs, but I can tell my observation has hit home.

'Jealous? Of you?'

She sounds mocking, but the more I think about it the more I'm sure I'm right. She's so used to being the one that all the boys fancy, the one that has all the sexual escapades while I'm just there in the background, the reliable, quiet friend who's never any threat. But now she's been dumped, and I'm going out with the hottest boy we've ever seen.

I don't voice my thoughts, I just sigh and curl my legs up underneath me. Everything and everyone around me is changing too much, too fast. It's like the ground shifting beneath my feet.

'It's just not like you,' she says.

'What you mean is, you want me to stay the same. You and Mum. You're always teasing me about not having a boyfriend, being a prude, and now that I've met someone and I'm happy you don't like it.'

'You don't look very happy,' she points out. I lift my head defiantly.

'Well, I am, and as my friend you should be pleased for me. Joe really loves me.'

Dannii gives that mocking little laugh again and it makes me want to slap her.

'Is that what he told you to get you into bed? God, Ash, you're so naive.'

'He said it afterwards,' I retort, trying to ignore the little slither of doubt that she's planted in my mind. I know he meant it and I'm not going to let her ruin this for me.

'Look,' I say, trying to calm down. I don't want to argue with her too. 'I know you're upset because of Dean and everything but I really need your support, Dan. Mum's being horrid and this is the first real relationship I've had and I wanted to talk to you about it.'

I try to smile at her, wanting my best friend back, wanting to sit and giggle and gossip about my news in the way I thought we would, but the smile she gives me back looks tight and forced.

'I'm sorry,' she says, though she doesn't sound it at all. 'It's just that it all seems so strange. Don't take this the wrong way, babe, but well, everyone's saying it.'

'Saying what?'

'Wondering what he sees in you. I mean, you're so different from each other. Have you seen the pictures of his ex on Facebook? She's all blonde and model looking.

People are saying he must be on the rebound, or he's just using you. I just don't want you to get hurt.'

She gives me what I think is supposed to be a sympathetic look, but I don't miss the little flash of triumph in her eyes as I recoil, hurt, at her words. I know she's just trying to upset me, after all the only people that could be talking about Joe and me are Dannii and her many hangers-on, and Joe thinks I'm beautiful, I know he does. Still, the image of his ex, blonde and beautiful, springs to my mind and I feel sick. The fact that that description also fits Dannii doesn't escape me either. I gasp as I realise exactly what her problem is.

'You're just upset that he doesn't fancy you, aren't you? That's what this is.' I shake my head, feeling betrayed, but Dannii just smirks at me.

'What makes you think he doesn't?' she looks straight at me, her eyes challenging, and my stomach turns over.

'What's that supposed to mean?'

I'm dreading what she's about to say, but she drops her eyes and says, 'Nothing. I'm just saying, that's all.' But I'm not convinced. Not at all.

'Just go,' I say flatly. 'I can't deal with this right now.'

Dannii widens her eyes, all hurt and protesting innocence. I'd feel guilty if I hadn't seen her pull this look a thousand times before, usually on some guy she's manipulating.

'I'm just trying to be a friend, Ash, just being honest. You're so infatuated with Joe, and I don't want to see you being taken advantage of.'

'He's not Dean,' I snap, and think and I'm not like you, but I don't say it. It occurs to me that lately, there's too much I'm not saying to people. Dannii looks like she's about to get bitchy again.

'Just stop,' I say. 'I don't want to fight. I need to be alone for a bit okay?'

She shrugs and picks up her bag.

'Okay, well, you know where I am if you need me.'

I'm about to say thank you, wondering if she really is just looking out for me and I'm being a total cow, when she says breezily on the way out the door;

'I was going to invite you to a party tonight but you're grounded aren't you? I think Dean and Joe are going. I'll text you later.'

She shuts the door behind her with a smirk, knowing her barb has hit home. Now I'll sit here all night, mulling over her comments about Joe and wondering if he's at some party. I should just phone him and tell him what's gone on, but I don't want to talk to anyone right now. I was so happy earlier and now everything feels ruined, and if Dannii does turn out to be right about Joe then I don't want to know. I turn my phone off and bury my face in the pillow, wondering how everything can go so wrong so quickly.

Chapter Seven

The next morning I turn my phone on to three missed calls off Joe, one from Dannii, one from Rianne, one from my dad and two texts off Joe. The first one 'love you beautiful' makes my insides jump but the second has me sinking again, 'Are you okay? Dannii said you had a massive row with your mum?' which implies he was with Dannii last night, or at least spoke to her. I need to see him, hold him, and reassure myself that the other night wasn't all a dream. That Mum and Dannii are wrong.

I dress quickly for my class this morning, throwing my hair up in a ponytail as I'm at work in the cafe this afternoon and head downstairs. I can hear Mum's in her studio and I try to get out without having to speak to her but she comes into the hall just as I'm putting my pumps on. She looks like she's been crying too.

We just stand there looking at each other before she holds her arms out and I run into them like a kid, burying my face in her shoulder. I'm as tall as her now, but she strokes my hair and shushes me like she used to when I was little and I'd fell over.

'I'm sorry. I was horrible,' I say. Mum wipes my eyes and smiles.

'I was pretty horrible too. If you really love this boy, then perhaps it's time I met him?'

My jaw drops.

'Really? Oh, Mum, thank you.'

I throw my arms around her again and she hugs me back quickly this time before stepping away, her face serious again.

'But tonight it's about us okay? I want you back straight from school.'

'College,' I protest with a sigh. 'And I've got work after.'

'Well, whatever you call it, but come straight home after the cafe. I'm doing dinner. For the three of us.'

Great. That means Dad. But if I want them to accept Joe, I suppose I'm going to have to deal with it so I force a smile.

'Okay. I'll be back about six.'

I walk to the bus with a confusion of emotions whirring around inside me. I'm still upset about Dannii and her attitude and although I'm desperate to see Joe part of me is almost nervous too. Things have changed between us, and what if Danni's right? What if he isn't as keen now, whereas I'm madly in love? But then I think of his smile when he looked down at me and told me he loved me and try to push Dannii's nasty words from my mind. She's just jealous, I remind myself. I should probably feel a bit sorry for her.

Right on cue my phone rings. Joe. I take a deep breath and answer it, feeling a spread of warmth in my body at the sound of his voice. He sounds so sexy on the phone, all deep and mature.

'Hey, babe. I was trying to get hold of you last night. What's happened?'

I tell him about my row with Mum, editing the part where I made Joe sound like a candidate for Crimewatch. I don't mention my row – if that's really what it was – with Dannii.

'The good news is, you're invited round to meet her. If you want to,' I add, wondering if he might think it a bit soon for the whole 'meet my mother' scenario. But he sounds really pleased.

'I'd love to. I was beginning to think you were ashamed of me,' he says lightly, but I'm glad he can't see my face as his words make me blush. 'What's the bad news?'

'Dinner with Mum and Dad tonight. 'Just the three of us.' Can't wait,' I say sarcastically.

'Can you get out after?'

'Hopefully. I've been dying to see you. So what did you do last night?'

'I went round Dean's, he had a few people there. I was calling you to see if you were coming. Dannii was there, she told me about the row with your mum.'

'Is she back on with Dean then?'

I hope he says yes, then maybe she will stop being such a cow about Joe and me. I know Dannii, she gets bitchy when she's upset.

'Well, that's what I thought earlier on in the evening, because they were kissing and stuff, but then they ended up screaming at each other and she went off home with this other guy that was there. Dean was raging, I had to stop him driving after them.'

I roll my eyes. This is typical Dannii drama, so hopefully things will go back to normal. At least she wasn't throwing herself all over Joe.

But then I can't help thinking, would he even tell me if she was?

I ring off, telling him I'll try to get out later. He wishes me luck with the whole family dinner thing, and he sounds so genuine I feel bad for doubting him. He's given me absolutely no reason to be anything but over the moon, but maybe that's the problem. When something seems too good to be true, isn't that usually because it is? Look at my parents, together for all those years, each other's first love and then pow, gone. The fact that they're rekindling things seems more like stupidity than true love to me.

Not surprisingly, classes drag and work drags even more. I'm dreading dinner, yet at the same time desperate to get it over and done with so I can go and see Joe.

Breakfast yesterday seems like an age away.

I'm so scatter brained at the cafe that I drop a whole tray of cutlery and give people the wrong orders twice. In the end Becky lets me go half an hour early, rolling her eyes at me.

'You're sure you don't need help cleaning up?' I ask gratefully as I hang up my apron. She shakes her head vehemently. 'Absolutely not.' She's probably worried I'll accidentally set fire to the place or something.

I text Mum to let her know I'm on my way home and set off, telling myself that I'm going to be pleasant and act pleased for them, but my stomach's in knots. Will she let him move back in? They might think it's what I want, for us all to be back together, when that couldn't be more wrong.

There's no sign of Dad's car as I walk up our drive, and I'm quite glad I'm home first. I take a deep breath as I walk in the front door.

'I'm home!' I shout unnecessarily but determined to seem cheerful. Mum comes to greet me out of the kitchen.

She looks beautiful. Dressed in a simple white dress with her hair all curly around her shoulders and some grey stuff round her eyes that really brings out the colour, she looks like a film star. There's a flush to her cheeks and a light in her eyes that has nothing to do with make-up. I sigh inwardly as she hugs me and leads me into the kitchen, plastering a big smile on my face to greet my dad with.

Except it's not my dad that's sitting at our kitchen table.

'Ashley, this is Matt,' Mum says, as excited as a puppy. I just stare, my mouth hanging open, totally confused.

'Where's Dad?' Is she cheating on him?

Mum frowns, looking as perplexed as I feel.

'Why would your dad be here? I mean, we're on good

terms, but it's not quite appropriate, Ash.'

The guy at the table has a frozen smile on his face as he looks back and forth between Mum and me, clearly unsure what to say. Then he gets up and offers me his hand.

'Pleased to meet you sweetheart. Although I feel like I already know you, Keira talks about you that much.'

I take his hand, staring at it as if he's got six fingers or something, and then sit down, wondering if I've entered some kind of weird alternate reality.

'And I'm so sorry about the other day,' he continues, 'we weren't expecting you back.' He looks embarrassed.

And finally, I get it. It never was Dad.

My eyes sweep over Matt. He has a similar build to my father and the same dark wavy hair…it would have been an easy mistake to make just from glimpsing the back of his head. He's better looking than Dad though and, I realise, younger. Late twenties to thirty maybe.

Wow. Go Mum.

I feel weirdly proud of her.

Turns out they've met through work, the latest project of Mum's; she's illustrating his books. As I sit and watch them I see how well they get on, how they bounce off each other and how happy she is, and I can't believe I ever thought it was Dad. Turns out her and Matt have been seeing each other for a while, but she wanted to make sure it was serious before she introduced us.

'We don't all like to rush things,' she says, a twinkle in her eye, but I know she's making a point about Joe and me and resist the temptation to stick my tongue out at her. Not a good look, especially if I want her to believe I'm having a mature, grown-up relationship.

Matt seems pretty cool though I can't help feeling a bit wary, but it's definitely, definitely better than the conclusions I'd jumped to. And if Mum's happy, she's more likely to accept Joe.

She won't accept everything though. I ask her if she minds if I leave them to it to go and see him and encouraged by her happy acceptance of that, I try to push it a bit.

'I could stay over, I'll give you his address? Then you and Matt can have some time on your own.'

Matt grins at me, obviously thinking that's a great idea, but Mum's face shuts down instantly, and she goes from happy loved-up young woman to stern parent in an instant, crossing her arms over her chest.

'No. Absolutely not.'

Her tone brooks no argument whatsoever. I pout at her, but she shakes her head firmly.

'No, Ash. At least, not until I've met him and got to know him myself. Back by twelve please.'

I sigh, but decide not to push it too far in case she tries grounding me again.

I quickly shower and change into a cute zebra print dress that Dannii gave me but I've never worn, trying to get my hair to curl and flow round my shoulders like Mum's. It ends up looking more like I've been electrocuted, so I give up and put it in a messy bun with a few wispy curls around my face. Some eyeliner and lip-gloss and I'm done. I inspect myself in front of the full-length mirror in the hall and can't help thinking I look pretty good. Okay I might not be blonde and busty and leggy like Dannii, but I think I look pretty hot. I can't wait to see Joe.

Mum offers me a lift and I hesitate, then accept. After all, I've already told her he lives on the Estate.

'I hope you don't go walking around here on your own,' she frowns as we drive down a street with more boarded up houses than lived in ones.

'He walks me most of the way back,' I assure her. 'And

you've never moaned about me visiting Rianne.'

She nods, conceding my point but still looks uncertain and so I jump out of the car as swiftly as possible, air kissing her cheek. She gives a little wave, still not looking too happy, but thankfully she drives off without saying anything or giving me any lectures. I hope her invitation to Joe won't result in her interrogating him over the dinner table.

'Have fun with Matt,' I call after her, and satisfied that I've made my point I knock on Joe's door, feeling the usual fizz of excitement.

His eyes widen when he opens the door and he looks me up and down with undisguised appreciation.

'Wow, you look gorgeous,' he says, pulling me towards him for a kiss.

The warm crush of his mouth chases away any lingering doubts that were still lurking, and my body thrills to his now familiar touch as if it recognises him instantly. He's warm and smells of aftershave and shower gel, with just a slight lingering metallic undertone of engine oil. I mould myself into him, letting my world narrow down to just consist of Joe and me.

We finally break away from each other and he holds the door wide for me to come in, playfully squeezing my bum as I walk past. 'So how did the reunion dinner go? I thought you might be a bit upset, to be honest, so I'm guessing it was all okay?'

'It wasn't exactly a reunion.' I giggle, and tell him about Matt. We're both laughing by the time I've finished.

'You're a dope,' he says with affection and ruffles my hair as we go to sit down.

'It's funny, because if I had just known from the start she had a new guy I might have been worried about it, but now I'm just so relieved it's not Dad.' Even as I say it I feel a bit sorry for my dad though after his admission the other week about still loving her.

I look at Joe and don't even want to think about how losing him would feel.

'I thought we could watch a film or something,' he shouts over from the kitchenette. There's a bottle of wine in the fridge Steph said we can have, if you want it. She's out at bingo.'

'Are you trying to get me drunk?' I tease. He smirks at me in a way that makes me blush all the way down to my groin.

'Do I need to?'

I debate throwing a cushion at him, but as he's now got glasses in his hand I decide against it. He comes over and hands me a drink of white wine that makes me pucker my mouth as I sip it. It's really dry, but I don't want to hurt his feelings so I try and look enthusiastic.

I needn't have bothered as Joe sits down, takes a swig and promptly spits it back out.

'Urgh, that's foul,' he grimaces.

'It's not the best,' I admit, laughing as Joe runs for a glass of water.

'I don't even like wine.'

'Why offer it then?'

He looks sheepish.

'I thought it would be romantic.'

He actually blushes as he says that and it's so cute I want to kiss him.

Eventually we end up curled up together on the sofa watching a teen horror, which is kind of crap but I pretend it's scarier than it is so that I can curl up closer and bury my head in his shoulder. And we drink beer.

I try to concentrate on the film, which he seems engrossed in – probably something to do with the overkill on hot bikini wearing girls – but just being next to him is distracting. Lying with my head on his shoulder I can smell his clean boy smell and feel the warmth of his body, and it takes a lot of self-control not to start nuzzling his neck or nipping at his earlobe. His arm's round me and his hand on my leg but he makes no other move to touch me other than the occasional quick kiss when there's a dull moment in the film. By the time it's coming to an end I'm practically itching with frustration. Is that normal? I mean, I've been not a virgin for less than two days and now getting naked with him seems to be all I can think about.

Joe seems completely oblivious.

'Good film, wasn't it? I've got the sequel if you want to put it on?'

'I've got to be home by twelve,' I point out, and his face falls.

'You should have said, I thought you were staying the night.'

Well, I suppose that explains why he was more interested in the film.

'I think Mum wants to meet you before she'll be cool with that. I could have said I was staying at Dannii's, but after the row we had yesterday I don't want to cause any more trouble.' I leave out the part about Dannii not being my favourite person right now.

'Yeah, you're probably right. It's going to feel awkward now that she found that stuff.' Joe grimaces and for the first time I realise all this is probably hard for him to. He's got to meet my mum knowing she's just found out we're sleeping together and is none too pleased about it. Thinking about it, he's probably glad himself that my dad isn't completely back on the scene.

'Does she know?' he asks abruptly and I don't quite get what he means.

'Well, she found the condoms and I told her I'd stayed here so...'

'No,' he cuts me off impatiently. 'I mean about me. About my record.'

I nod, and his face hardens. Not for the first time I kick myself for yesterday's little outburst.

'Why?' he demands, looking angry now and moving away so he's pressed into the corner of the sofa. 'Now she's already going to have a bad opinion of me. Wouldn't it be better if I had met her first?'

'She won't have a bad opinion of you, she's really not judgemental like that.' God I hope I'm right. She was so angry and completely judgemental yesterday that I'm thinking she's perhaps not as laidback as I thought. Surely she'll love him, how could she not?

'I'm sorry,' I say quietly as he continues to look angry, and wonder if we're about to have our first row. But his face clears and he puts his arm back round me, tipping my chin up to look at him with his other hand.

'It's alright, babe,' he says softly, though I can tell he's anxious about meeting her now. I go to apologise again but he lowers his face to mine, and finally kisses me like I've been waiting for him to all night.

We kiss for ages, all thoughts of parents and the past forgotten, until we end up splayed out on the settee with him lying between my thighs and his hands inside my shirt. At some point either he or I has taken his top off and I run my hands over the taut broadness of his shoulders, loving the feel of him. When his hands go up under my dress and tug at my knickers I pull away gasping.

'I didn't bring a condom,' I say cursing myself. I was so busy admiring myself in the mirror I didn't even think about it. He groans in frustration, pushing his hips into me so I can feel exactly how much he wants me.

'Haven't you started that Pill yet?'

He moves gently against me, starting a low thrumming in my body that doesn't care about contraception or anything else other than feeling him inside me again. I close my eyes as if blocking out the sight of his desire filled eyes is going to help, but it just makes me more aware of his body pushing against mine. I shift to the side to relieve some of the pressure, but it has the opposite effect on him as he makes a low growling noise against my neck.

'Not until next week.'

'Damn, Ash.' I can hear the need in his voice.

We kiss again and I feel that delicious warmth spreading through my body. I want to lose myself in him and I know if one of us doesn't pull away soon I'll be making another trip to the doctors tomorrow.

I don't know which of us does it first but we pull away from each other, breathing heavily and adjusting our clothes, Joe taking a peek up my skirt as I pull it down with no shame at all.

'Wow, that was intense,' he says, and I nod. Intense doesn't even begin to describe it. Joe looks up at the clock.

'You'll have to leave in about an hour if you want to get home in time anyway, and I don't want to have sex and then boot you out.' He grins at me and I poke him playfully in the ribs.

'Cheeky. More like I don't want to have sex and then just leave. You might feel used.'

We laugh, which breaks some of the tension, and end up watching a comedy on the TV. Nothing sexual, which is probably just as well. I lie on Joe with my head on his chest, our legs entwined. I feel safe and happy. Crazy how much can change in just one day.

The rollercoaster ride of emotions I've experienced over the last few days must have taken its toll because before I know it I've dozed off and Joe is shaking me awake.

'How long have I been asleep?' I ask, looking at the clock and feeling a wave of disappointment as I see it's time to go.

'I was tempted to let you sleep so that you had to stay over, but figured your mum would then just hate me,' he says. I sigh, knowing he's right, and drag my still sleepy limbs up and off the sofa.

Walking back the Estate looks almost pretty in the moonlight, in a kind of spooky way. We're just approaching the park, hand in hand and me yawning uncontrollably when I see a figure coming in our direction on the other side of the street. As they get nearer I realise who it is and tense automatically, my hand gripping Joe's.

Jason, walking with that cocky swagger some guys adopt. His eyes sweep over us and even from across the road I can see the hostility in his gaze. Joe stares back, his face completely impassive, until Jason drops his eyes and continues on his way. For all of his menacing air, I know he's wary of Joe, and although that gives me kind of a thrill, knowing that he could protect me, it worries me too. Is his past really behind him? I wonder how he would react if he was in a similar situation now. I can sense rather than feel how his body has gone tight, like he's ready to pounce. Then he turns and smiles at me and I tell myself to stop being stupid. Over dramatizing things again.

Joe walks me home, right to the end of the street as it's so late and I wonder if I should bring him in, but it's pretty late and we've both got to get up. Hopefully after he's met Mum she'll be okay with me staying over, and in any case I'm eighteen in a few months.

But for now we kiss goodbye on the end of the street like we're still in Year Ten and I walk down my road looking back over my shoulder to see if he looks back himself.

He does.

Hugging myself in delight I let myself in, fuss the dog for ten minutes and then go upstairs, wide awake now. Seeing Mum's door ajar and her reading lamp on, I knock lightly, wondering if Matt's still here.

'Come in,' she calls. She's alone, sitting up in bed with a book in her hand. I squint at the cover and laugh when I see what it is. Mum's a crime and thriller fan and always teases me for my love of old fashioned romances, but in her hands is a book of mine, all virgins with heaving bosoms and dashing highwaymen. She must have it bad.

'Sit down,' she pats the bed and I sit on the edge, remembering back to when I was little and I would wake up in the night and creep in next to her. It happened a few times after Dad left too.

'Did you have a nice time?'

The way she says it, I know it's not what she really wants to ask and I sigh. We're going to 'talk' I just know it. I decide to just plunge right in.

'We didn't have sex again, and when we do, I'll be fully protected. And no, he's not pressuring me into it.' If anything, I think I want it as much as if not more than he does. But I'm not telling Mum that.

She just nods slowly at my words, her eyes sweeping my face as if assessing me and I squirm under the scrutiny. Finally she gives a sharp, satisfied nod.

'Okay, Ashley. I don't like it, but you were going to grow up sometime. I'm just surprised you didn't talk to me about it beforehand.'

She looks hurt, which makes me feel like crap, so I tell her the truth.

'I wanted to. I was worried that you wouldn't approve of Joe and I knew there was something going on with you.' I pause, and she jumps in, blaming herself.

'I was distracted because of Matt' —she looks horrified— 'and you felt you couldn't talk to me.'

'No,' I say quickly, hating the look of self-recrimination in her eyes. 'It's not that. I was avoiding talking to you about anything because I thought, well I thought you were getting back with Dad.'

I expect her to burst out laughing or even get cross but instead her eyes fill with tears. I don't understand until she reaches over and pats my hand.

'I'm sorry, sweetheart. You must be so disappointed. I had no idea that Rob returning would get your hopes up like that.'

Oh God, she thinks I wanted them to get back together? I shake my head vehemently.

'No, you don't get it. I didn't want you to be back together. I was so worried, I thought it would just happen all over again.'

I have to blink to stop my own eyes tearing up, but Mum looks relieved.

'I'm really happy for you, Matt seems great,' I assure her, and a thought occurs to me. 'Does Dad even know?'

'A little. I haven't made too much of an issue of it, what with his situation with Anya.'

Which shows how decent she is really; you couldn't have blamed her for rubbing her happiness right in his face. At that vindictive little thought I feel instantly ashamed. It's not Mum who is still bitter about him leaving, it's me. I rub my face, feeling tired again. I'm not sure I can cope with all these revelations. Mum seems to notice and holds her hand out. I hesitate only for a second before snuggling up into the crook of her arm.

'Tell me about this Joe then,' she murmurs against my hair. So I do. I tell her how hot he is, how he makes me feel both special and safe and how the world seems more vivid with him around. Mum just listens.

'So what's all this about the prison sentence?' she probes gently. I tell her as much as I know, continuing to sing Joe's praises, trying to paint him as a hero almost and ignoring the twinge of doubt I had earlier when we walked past Jason.

'So you're not worried about his temper?' she asks as if reading my mind. But I catch the edge in her voice and realise with horror what she means.

'No, Mum,' I say firmly. 'Joe would never hurt me, not like that.' And instinctively I know it to be true.

'He's worried you're going to judge him because of it,' I tell her. 'But I told him you're not like that.'

She gives a little snort at that.

'Because by telling me that you know I'll now go out of my way to seem non-judgemental? Very clever, Ash. But I promise I'll take him as I find him, okay? It's never easy for a mother to meet her daughter's first boyfriend; you're not my little girl anymore.'

It wasn't easy for me to catch her in bed with a guy either, I think but bite back the retort. I guess we both have some coming to terms with things to do.

I lie with her for a while then kiss her on the cheek and go to bed, texting goodnight to Joe and falling asleep before I hear my phone beep with his reply.

The next morning Dannii knocks my door to walk to class with me, as we're both in at the same time. She doesn't even mention our row the other day, just chatters on about what a jerk Dean is and how she's now got her sight sets on this other guy she met at his place, just as Joe had told me.

'But won't that just wind Dean up more?' I point out. Dannii just shrugs and starts talking about something else. I wonder if this new boy is in fact nothing but a tool to do exactly that; wind Dean up. I think Dannii is a lot more into him than she's letting on, and is actually pretty gutted about their break up. Of course, she'll never admit it.

'So you and Joe are back on?' she cuts into my thoughts with an abruptness that makes me think she's really wanted to ask me this all along.

'We were never off,' I say, not missing the quick frown that she quickly replaces with an interested smile. 'But yeah, things are great.'

She links her arm through mine. We used to walk around school like this on our lunch break, making the younger students walk around us.

'That's good then. We'll all have to go out again soon.'

I mumble something non-committal, not sure why the idea bothers me so much. After all she's trying to be nice.

As we get to the sixth form block we hug and air kiss, Dannii going off to Media Studies and me to English. I watch her as she sashays down the corridor, her hips swinging as she passes a trio of guys. As one they turn their heads to watch her and a twinge of jealousy gnaws at my gut. Never before have I ever seen Dannii as any kind of rival, and yet since I've met Joe there seem to be under-currents in our friendship and if I'm honest, they're not all coming from her. I shake my head at myself as I walk into class. It's hardly Dannii's fault she's gorgeous.

Today's lesson is actually pretty interesting, and I get through a whole hour before realising I haven't sat and daydreamed about Joe once. Of course as soon as I think it he's on my mind for the rest of the morning. He rings at break, and as always the sound of his voice gets my tummy fluttering.

'Hey, sexy,' he says and I blush like a schoolgirl, 'want to meet up this afternoon? It's my half day at work and I've got college tonight.'

I'd forgotten he wasn't working this afternoon. My heart

pace picks up as I contemplate seeing him earlier than anticipated.

'Sure, I'm finished at half one.'

As soon as he's gone I run to the toilets to check my hair and apply more mascara, wishing I had put nicer underwear on and then blushing at my own thoughts. With any luck, it won't be staying on for too long. I'm almost hungry to feel his hands on me again.

My phone beeps with a message just as I pick it up to put it on silent and my fingers rush to open it, expecting it to be from Joe, but it's Rianne, which is a surprise because she's not really in the habit of texting.

Can you pop round today? Need to tell you something.

That sounds odd, but I try to tell myself she probably needs a friend and is just stressed out with motherhood. Or maybe she and Mitch are having problems. Yet in spite of my assurances to myself I can't shake the notion that whatever she needs to tell me, I'm not going to like it. The ominous feeling hangs over me for the rest of class, taking the edge off my excitement at seeing Joe. I decide I'll pop in on my way to his house, and ignore the little voice telling me not to, in case it's bad news.

In case whatever she is about to tell me is going to change everything.

Chapter Eight

The sense of foreboding is still there as I stand on Rianne's doorstep, waiting for her to answer. I've been standing here for a few minutes and I'm about to ring the bell again when I see her outline through the glass.

'Sorry,' she says as she answers and ushers me in. 'I just had to change Gabe, he's been sick all over himself.'

I smile at little Gabriel and he rewards me with a gummy grin, then loudly fills his nappy. The stink hits me nearly straight away. Rianne rolls her eyes, sighing.

'That's the third time today. He had his jabs yesterday and his tummy's playing right up,' she says as I sit down and she lays the baby on his changing mat.

'He seems happy enough,' I observe, watching him beam at his mum, kicking his fat little legs.

'Well, he's had a good sleep, but he's going through nappies like anything.' Rianne wrinkles her nose as she puts the dirty nappy into a little plastic bag and ties it before throwing it into the kitchen bin with what is clearly a well-practiced shot. With the required baby talk out of the way she leaves Gabriel to lie on the mat shoving a teddy bear into his mouth and sits next to me.

The bad feeling comes back. She's not quite meeting my eyes and in an instant I know, I just somehow know that whatever this is it's about Joe. And it's not going to be good.

'Spit it out then, Ri, what do you need to tell me?'

She looks at the floor as if she's considering how to tell me then meets my eyes and says in a matter of fact tone, 'I heard a rumour that Dannii and Joe were kissing at some party. I don't know how true it is so I haven't mentioned it to anyone other than you. It might just be gossip, but I thought you should know.'

She sounds so reasonable it takes me a few minutes to grasp what it is that she's actually said. Then it hits me and my stomach lurches.

'At a party?'

My body has gone all still, even my mouth struggling to form the words. All I can think is, *I knew it.* I've not wanted to admit it to myself, just as I didn't want to face what I thought was going on with my parents, but I know there's something not right where Dannii and Joe are concerned. I had thought – or hoped – I was just being insecure.

I press my hand to my stomach as it lurches again.

'Where was this party?' I ask again, fixating on that one detail, remembering Dannii's casual remark about a party at Dean's. Where Joe would be. When I was stuck in my room.

The night after I'd given him my virginity.Looking down at my hands I see they're shaking, but I feel weirdly detached from them, as if I'm in someone else's body.

But Rianne's answer isn't what I expect.

'At her house, when her brother came back. I don't know exactly when, like I said it might just be gossip.'

My heart sinks to meet my stomach.

'I was there that night. I stayed with him,' I say, but I know that doesn't make it not true. Because there was the ten minutes or so when they had both disappeared, and then reappeared within seconds of each other, but it was all forgotten about because of the standoff with Jason and his mates.

'Who did you hear this off?' I ask, hoping that just maybe this is something to do with Jason, a way for him to get back at us, and not true at all. But I'm just clutching at straws.

'Mitch was in the pub and he saw Michael. He told him,

but he hadn't seen it himself, his friend told him later on that night.'

No, I remember, Michael had been in the kitchen with some girl. So it might still not be true, which would be a lot more comforting if my memory wasn't assailed with all the little things I've noticed, little puzzles that are now coming together to make a very clear picture. The way she was all over him at the cinema, his face for just a second when we spoke about her at the garage, and Dannii's comment, with her perfectly plucked eyebrow raised: 'What makes you think he doesn't?'

Something's happened, I know it has, and the knowledge is too much. It's like a physical blow, my body curling up as if to protect myself from it. Rianne looks horrified.

'Ash, I'm so sorry. I wish I'd never told you, but I thought if you found out from someone else and I'd known the whole time…' she trails off and I see the threat of tears in her eyes.

'No, you did the right thing,' I say, my voice hollow. 'I would have done the same.' I try and smile at her and she looks relieved, but it's a more a grimace than a smile, my facial muscles revolting. All I want to do is scream and scream and scream, but it isn't Rianne's fault. At least one of my friends is loyal.

'I can't believe her,' I say, and my voice is a whisper now. Rianne pats my knee, an awkward gesture that I know is meant to be comforting.

'Dannii's just out for herself,' she says quietly. 'She soon dropped me when I wasn't available to hang out with her all the time. She's barely seen Gabe.'

Before this I would have tried to defend Dannii. I always have, and for this? A wave of anger makes me ball my fists.

'I have to go,' I say, standing up. Rianne stands up with

me, looking worried.

'Don't do anything crazy; remember, we don't even know if it's true.' But even she doesn't sound convinced.

My limbs feel numb as I hug Rianne goodbye and start to walk to Joe's, wondering what the hell I'm going to say to him. What I'm going to do. I understand why people refer to betrayal as being stabbed in the back because just the thought of it makes my insides twist painfully. I feel fragile, like I'm about to break.

Sill, by the time I reach Joe's I've managed to take a few deep breaths and compose myself a bit, but my heart's a lump in my throat as he answers the door, looking as hot as ever, his face lighting up when he sees me.

'Babe!' he wraps me in a hug that I return stiffly, holding my breath because I don't want to catch the scent of him as my face is crushed into his neck, don't want to crumble and dissolve into tears right on his doorstep. He steps back with a frown but doesn't say anything. Steph is there, waving over at me. I wave back, letting out my breath in a sigh that's almost a moan. Joe looks worried.

'What's wrong?'

'I'll tell you in a minute,' I say in a hushed tone and Joe looks over at Steph and back at me.

'Okay, well, come upstairs. I need to grab a shower, then you can tell me. Is it your mum again?'

He takes my sullen shrug as assent and leads me up the stairs. In his room he strips off and ties the towel round his waist without any self-consciousness at all and in spite of myself I have to look. I still feel the familiar stab of desire at the sight of him but now it's accompanied by a nauseous empty feeling that has me turning my head away and blinking back tears. Joe kisses me on the head before he goes into the bathroom.

'I won't be a minute, babe.' He sounds so concerned, I

think bitterly, no doubt thinking I've come running to him with my silly family dramas again and I'll be straight in his bed again afterwards. Because if this is true, if anything has happened between him and Dannii then it was all a lie, he can't really love me at all and I've done the very thing I've never wanted to; given my virginity up to someone who will just throw it away.

It can't be true. Oh God, don't let it be true.

I wait for him, my hands shaking again, running through all the possible scenarios in my mind and not one of them has a happy ending. Except the one where all of this is a bad dream and I wake up and Joe and I are still in love and Dannii is still my best friend.

A shrill beep makes me jump and I look in its direction, spotting Joe's phone on the table near his bed. I pick it up and draw in a sharp breath as I see the little notification that tells him he has received a picture message. And from someone called 'D'.

Knowing I shouldn't but equally knowing I have to I click on the button to open it, my heart pounding in my chest.

As the image appears before me a wave of nausea so strong hits me that I feel dizzy and sit down, still staring at the picture.

Dannii. Smiling provocatively at the camera, her silky hair down all over her shoulders, not quite covering her boobs. Her naked boobs.

I put the phone back where it was, tearing my eyes away from the photo, my mind struggling to process what this means. More than a quick snog at a party. He could be sleeping with her too, comparing me, the virgin, to my hotter and more experienced best friend. The thought makes me burn with shame imagining them curled up together, laughing at me. I don't want to believe it, not when I was so sure of him, so sure he meant all he had said. But the evidence is staring me in the face.

I hear Joe coming back in the room and I stand up, hoisting my bag on my shoulder.

'What are you doing?'

'I'm going,' I answer, not looking at him but at a point over his shoulder, 'and I'm not coming back.'

Joe steps towards me, holding a hand out as if to touch me and I recoil sharply. He drops his hand, the hurt evident in his eyes. Good. And in that moment I decide I'm not going to confront him, not going to rage and cry and plead with him for answers. My anger settles in my stomach like a hot hard ball and still refusing to meet his eyes I push past him.

'Ash, what the hell? Why are you being like this?'

'Leave me alone,' I toss back over my shoulder, catching his eyes long enough to see the raw pain in his eyes, 'this was a mistake.'

I storm down the stairs and straight out of the door, not stopping to say goodbye to Steph and ignoring Joe's calls for me to come back. I half expect him to follow me, but he doesn't.

He calls me when I reach the end of his street but I reject it and dial Dannii's number instead, her cheerful voice when she answers bringing with it a fresh surge of anger. I wonder if she's got dressed.

'Hi, babe, what are you up to tonight?'

'I've just been to Rianne's,' I bite out, 'and I know Dannii. I know.'

'Know what?' she says, just the fraction of a second too late. She knows exactly what I mean.

'At your house that night? With Joe? You were seen.'

There's a sharp intake of breath and then silence, and my world comes crashing down around me. Part of me was hoping she would deny it, say it was all rubbish and spin me some story I could at least pretend to believe. Anything rather than face the horrible fact that my boyfriend is cheating on me with my best friend. For all I know it could have been going on before I had even met him.

'Ash, I'm so, so sorry,' she says, tearful. I'm crying now too but they're hot, angry tears.

'You bitch,' I hiss, cutting her off. She phones back almost instantly and I reject it as I had Joe's. I don't want to talk to either of them, don't want to hear apologies. How can there be an adequate apology for this? It's not like scratching someone's CD or wearing their clothes without asking. 'Ooops sorry, I didn't mean to snog your boyfriend.' Or whatever else they've been doing behind my back.

I walk back at twice my usual pace, my trainers thumping on the path in time with my racing heartbeat. I want to break into a jog, if only to relieve some of the tension in my body.

Just as I reach the park Joe phones again and this time I don't just reject it but turn it off completely. I'm so mad I barely even register that I'm walking through here alone for the first time since that night Jason and Adam were harassing me. I see two boys in caps and hoodies standing by the swings and as I get closer I see one of them is Adam's ferret faced friend. He smirks at me as I storm past.

'Not with your boyfriend today then?'

'I don't have a fucking boyfriend,' I snarl.

The wave of anger carries me home and I walk through my front door in record time. Mum isn't back and my anger subsides in an instant, leaving me feeling very, very alone.

I open the kitchen door and Sabre throws himself at me, tail wagging and tongue lolling. He calms down as I kneel down next to him, sensing my mood he cocks his head on one side and looks at me with those big doggy eyes, then nudges at me and licks my hand. I put my arms round his neck, breathing in the smell of his fur and he licks the side of my face. Normally I would find that disgusting and push him away but instead I bury my face in the ruff round his neck, holding onto him like a lifejacket, and I cry and cry and cry.

Chapter Nine

I don't go into class the next morning. In fact, I don't even bother to get out of bed. I leave my phone turned off and lie in bed, staring at the wall. Try as I might I can't make any sense of this. I try to think things through logically, but my mind's a mess, slipping away from the reality it doesn't want to grasp. Dannii and Joe. Joe and Dannii. Perhaps it was inevitable; after all there's no denying they're a better fit. The most popular girl in Year 13 and the hot new 'bad boy'. They could be characters in one of my stories. Girls like me only ever get the bit parts.

It's all too much. I feel both raw and empty as if someone's taken a scourer to the inside of me. Only every so often a wave of emotion hits me and I sob silently into my pillow, opening my mouth in a silent scream. It's like Dad leaving all over again; the sense of being abandoned, of wondering what I did wrong. For the first time I get a sense of what Mum must have gone through.

It's gone eleven before she pops her head in the door, her eyes widening as she takes in the sight of me.

'What on earth is the matter?' she crosses over to me, pressing a hand on my forehead. I shake her off.

'I'm not ill,' I sob and she squats beside me, peering into my face. I must look a mess, my face puffy and swollen.

'It's this Joe boy isn't it?'

She purses her lips, looking angry for a minute and I wish again that none of this was true. Only two nights ago I was singing his praises to her, desperate for her to approve.

'Get up and get dressed,' she says firmly, standing up and pulling the quilt off me to see me curled up in my dressing gown. I'll put the kettle on and you can tell me what's wrong. If you want to.' she adds. I can tell she's been trying to treat me less like a child lately and I love her for it, even though right now I wish I could crawl into her lap.

My arms and legs feel heavy as I drag on jeans and a vest, running a comb through my hair, which for once looks lank rather than fuzzy. My eyelids are like bee stings and my face blotchy. I give myself a look of disgust. No wonder Joe wanted Dannii. Even when she cries she looks great.

When I tell Mum what's happened and give voice to my self-loathing she surprises me by banging her coffee cup down on the table sharply.

'Stop talking like that; you're not a victim, stop feeling bloody sorry for yourself.'

I gape at her. Of course I'm a victim! But she continues in that no nonsense tone.

'You're not going to sit here whining and blaming yourself. You have done nothing wrong; they have. You are a beautiful intelligent girl, Ashley Evans, and to be quite honest, far too good for some young boy fresh out of jail.'

I almost bristle at her summation of Joe before I remember what he's done.

'Thanks.' I murmur, not really believing her. She's my mother, of course she thinks I'm wonderful.

'I suppose you're relieved,' I say. She looks shocked.

'Don't be stupid, the last thing I want is to see you this upset. Tell me exactly what's happened; do you know for sure that something has gone on between them?'

I tell her everything, from Rianne's recounting of it to seeing the topless picture to Dannii's tearful apology. When I've finished I'm crying again and Mum passes me a tissue, tapping her nails on the table. I notice she's got green paint on her hands.

'I've always expected something like this from that girl.'

'But we've been best friends for years,' I wail, the pain of her betrayal fresh again.

'But you haven't heard his side of it have you? Or hers really.'

I frown, not sure what she's getting at. It's pretty obvious something's gone on, and whether it's just a kiss and a picture or they're full on having sex doesn't make much difference, I realise. Either way they've crossed a line.

'I'm just saying, perhaps you should get all the facts before you decide what to do.'

It hasn't occurred to me that I even have any choices.

'They're probably together right now,' I say glumly, shutting my eyes against the mental picture of the two of them happy and smiling, hand in hand. Of course, that doesn't make it go away.

'Maybe,' she concedes, dipping her chin, 'but maybe not. Dannii rang the house phone for you earlier this morning. She sounded upset when I told her you were in bed.'

'Oh.' It makes no difference. Dannii might well grovel and cry, but she can't take it back. Neither of them can. Joe must have realised why I rushed out when he saw the picture message open on his phone. It occurs to me that by hiding and ignoring them both I've given them time to concoct a story together. How will I ever know the truth now?

'You need to face this,' Mum says firmly, 'not hide in your room.'

I sigh, taking a long swallow of coffee. I think she's being a bit unfair, I should be entitled to some time to wallow, but she's probably right. Taking a deep breath I go into the hall and use the house phone to call Dannii. She picks up after just one ring.

'Ashley?' she sobs. 'Oh, thank God, I've been trying to

get hold of you all morning.'

'I didn't want to talk to you.'

She starts crying harder so that it takes me a minute to understand what she's saying.

'I can't believe he could do this to me,' she wails.

'Who? Joe?'

'No,' she says impatiently, 'Dean.'

She's expecting me to care about her stupid arguments with Dean right now?

'I don't care about you and Dean,' I nearly shout into the phone, angry now at her selfishness and the sound of her crying. 'How could you go near Joe?' It's probably why Dean dumped her.

Dannii goes quiet, her sobs muffled.

'Are you in?' I ask, looking at the clock. She should be in class too.

'Yes.'

'I'll be there in a minute,' I say, replacing the phone. Mum gives me a thumbs up.

'I'll give you a lift,' she offers. It's not far at all to Dannii's, but I nod, grateful for the offer.

'You know, you should ask your dad to buy you a car. It's about time you started driving lessons,' she says as I get in the car. She's trying to distract me and give me something positive to think about I'm sure, but it would be a lot more convincing if not for the fact that she only took her own test when I was fourteen. Dad used to drive us everywhere.

'Joe loves cars,' I say, and tears come to my eyes again. So much for the change of topic. Mum drives the rest of the way in silence, but when we get to Dannii's she hugs me hard.

'Don't take any crap off her,' she warns me as I get out. I smile unconvincingly and steel myself for whatever I'm about to hear as I knock Dannii's door.

She almost drags me into the house, slamming the door shut as if she doesn't want anyone to see her.

'Have you seen them?' she hisses at me as we go up to her room. 'They're everywhere.'

I stare at her. Has the guilt driven her out of her mind?

'Dannii,' I say patiently as if I'm talking to a small child, 'what the hell are you going on about?'

'The photos!' She buries her head in her hands and when she looks back up she looks so distraught I have to stop myself going over and hugging her. Remember why you're here, I tell myself firmly.

'I'm so sorry,' she says through her tears, 'and I know you don't care about me and probably think I deserve it.'

'Deserve what?'

She looks at me in horror.

'You don't know? But Joe said you saw the picture.'

'I did,' I say through gritted teeth, 'on his phone.'

'Well, that's not just it. He's sent them to everyone. He's even put some of me in my underwear on Facebook!'

And the knowledge hits me like a blow to the head.

Dannii didn't send that picture to Joe. Dean did. Dean was 'D'. The relief is so strong I'm actually grinning, which makes Dannii cry even more.

'Why did you let him take pictures of you like that then?' I say, shaking my head at her stupidity.

'He said I looked hot, and it was fun. I just didn't think.'

It occurs to me this could all be a cover up, but looking at her stricken face I know she's telling me the truth.

'How can I ever face anyone again, ever?'

I bite back the comment that springs to my lips, which is that half of the local guys have probably seen her a lot more than topless anyway. It's a horrible thing that Dean's done, and if it's on Facebook she'll be in for a lot of teasing, especially from the legions of girls who have always been jealous of her. Dannii has been well and truly knocked off her pedestal. Although she kind of deserves it, I feel sorry for her too.

Then it hits me. I've been getting the wrong idea about a lot of things lately; Matt, the picture, am I wrong about Joe? Perhaps if it was just a kiss…but even so I could never trust them again.

'So what happened that night at the party? Tell me the truth Dannii please.' I'm calm now, prepared for whatever she's got to say. She chokes on a sob.

'I didn't mean to, it was just a stupid moment,' she says, and I feel my stomach twist into knots but I stay quiet and let her continue.

'I don't know what I was thinking, I mean I was with Dean. But we were all drinking. I didn't plan to do it Ash I swear. I'm horrible. I should never have tried to kiss him, I'm so sorry.'

I had closed my eyes, maybe against whatever she was going to reveal, and they snap open at that one word that causes a spark of hope to ignite.

She *tried* to kiss him? Only tried?

'I feel such an idiot,' she continues, blushing. 'He looked at me like I was scum.'

'He turned you down,' I state, finally understanding everything. For a second I feel elated, then I remember the way I stormed out on him. What have I done?

Dannii just continues to snuffle.

'I thought you were seeing each other,' I admit, and she looks at me in horror, 'I thought you sent him that picture.'

'Ash, no! I would never!'

'Never what? What if he'd kissed you back? That's obviously what you wanted. Isn't it?'

She drops her eyes and I sit down, feeling dejected again.

'Why?' I ask her. 'How could you?'

She starts crying again but I feel no pity for her now. If he had responded to her, how far would she have gone? Would she have taken him from me just to prove she could?

'I was right wasn't I, when I accused you of being jealous?'

Dannii is quiet for long enough that I think she's not going to answer, and when she does her voice is so quiet I have to lean forward to hear her.

'Yeah, I was jealous. You get the best of everything, you always do, and it's not fair.'

'Huh?' She's knocked me for six. 'What are you on about? I should be jealous of you! You're the pretty one, the popular one. I've always been invisible next to you.'

'I know,' she sniffs, proving that even humiliated and contrite, she's still Dannii, 'but only because you've always been a bit shy. You're just as pretty as me, loads of boys liked you at high school, you were just never interested.'

I shrug.

'That doesn't explain why you would be jealous. Is it just because of Joe? Because you like him?'

She shakes her head.

'I don't even really fancy him. He's hot, yeah, but too moody and serious for me. It was just that you get the best of everything else, all I get is the cool boyfriend, and then you had that too.'

I just don't get it. I look around at her room, filled with all the latest gadgets, a designer wardrobe, everything a girl could want. And her parents are still together.

'You've got everything,' I say. She snorts.

'You mean Mum and Dad buy me everything to make up for the fact that they want me out of their way? Your mum is amazing, the two of you are so close. And you're so clever. I can't even cope with college, I'm behind in everything.'

'I would have helped you if you'd asked,' I point out. She sits staring at her hands.

'That's not the point,' she says.

I kind of get it. After all I know now what jealousy feels like, how it twists inside you, but how could Dannii have felt like this for however long and never said anything? Unless…I think of all the times Dannii has teased me for being a prude and a swot and wonder if that's been behind her jibes all the time.

It's no excuse though. However envious I am of her face, her figure, her ability to effortlessly attract a man, I could never have done something like this.

'He must love you,' she points out.

'Why, because he managed to turn the luscious Dannii down? Get over yourself,' I snap, standing up. Her mention of Joe makes me desperate to get to him, to apologise for not talking to him, for not trusting him. The thought that it might be too late, that this has ruined everything, makes me look at Dannii in contempt. She doesn't seem to have a clue what she has done.

She sees I'm about to leave and pushes in front of me, her eyes desperate.

'Don't fall out with me, Ash. Say we can still be friends. It was just a stupid moment,' she begs, grabbing my arm. I shake my head.

'It's not as easy as that. I need to go and sort this mess out, if I can. You'll have to deal with Dean on your own. I'm sure you can make him take the pictures down, there's laws and things.'

I know I'm being harsh but I honestly couldn't care less about the exposure of Dannii's boobs. I just want to get to Joe. She moves out of my way, but she calls after me as I'm halfway down the stairs.

'Please, Ash, you're all I've got.'

I pause looking back at her and her face is so anguished that I can't help it, I do feel sorry for her.

'I'll call you later,' I promise, and she gives me a pathetic little smile before I rush out of the door.

I catch the bus to the garage, putting on some lip-gloss and trying unsuccessfully to do something with my hair. I have the usual butterflies at the prospect of seeing him, but they're tinged with apprehension rather than excitement as I have no idea how he will react to seeing me. He might be angry at me turning up at work, I think, and almost get back on the bus.

I needn't have worried, because he's not even there. The guy that whistled at me before is in the office and he looks up in surprise as I walk in.

'Joe phoned in sick today,' he says.

'Did he say what was wrong?' I ask, my heart hammering. This isn't like him at all, he loves his work. The mechanic shakes his head.

'Nah, but he said he would be in tomorrow. He's not had a day off before, maybe he's got the flu.'

He squints at me.

'You okay? You look upset.'

'Just tired,' I mumble, backing out of the door.

I have to wait another twenty minutes for the next bus that will take me near the park by the Estate, and I'm bouncing on the balls of my feet by the time it comes, wishing I had brought my phone. By the time I get to the park I'm flustered and panicking. What if he's not even there? He could have gone to a mates or to the pub or anything, and then if Steph's out too I'll have to get all the way back home before I can contact him.

I'm so engrossed in my own anxiety that when I first

walk into the park I don't even notice the fracas at the other end until a shout makes me look up. There's a handful of girls and a larger group of guys gathered around two others who look like they're about to have a fight. As I get a bit closer I see with a gasp who they are.

Jason, prowling menacingly in front of the other boy, shouting insults I can't hear. His rival just stands still glaring at him with the intense eyes and scornful mouth I would recognise from any distance.

Joe.

I break into a jog as the crowd of spectators huddle together so that for a few moments I can't see him. I shout his name but know he probably won't hear me above the excited chatter of the girls on the edge of the crowd and the shouted encouragement from Jason's goons. If they decide to jump in, Joe is going to get hurt.

As I finally reach them and start to push through the crowd I come face to face with Adam, who smirks at me.

'Hey, have you seen those photos going round of your mate? Told you she was a slag.'

'She's not a slag,' I say automatically. 'What's happening? Why are they fighting?'

Adam laughs.

'Because of you, of course. Joe came through the park earlier and Jason said he heard you two had split up.'

'And?' I demand, at the same time thinking if Joe was walking through the park he must have been on his way to see me.

'Jason said it was a free country for one of us to have a go,' Adam leers, and my stomach drops. Now I'm not so worried about Joe getting hurt as I am about him hurting someone else. He'll go back to prison, and it won't be the juvenile version this time.

'Joe!' I shout again and start to elbow my way through

until I'm on the inside of the crowd and just a few feet from Joe and Jason. He hears me and turns, startled.

'Ashley?'

I'm about to run to him, when Jason uses the distraction to make his move and his fist sails through the air.

Right into Joe's face.

Chapter Ten

I scream, and start forward, only to have Adam grab my arm.

'You'll embarrass him,' he hisses at me, and I glare at him, wondering why he's so bothered. I turn back still caught in his grip just in time to see Joe stumbling backwards, his hand to his mouth. When he takes it away there's blood on it.

'I'm calling the police,' says a girl next to me, and my eyes swivel to her in horror. What if they arrest Joe? But a lad next to her knocks it out of her hand.

'Don't be stupid, this is getting good,' he says. He has his own phone held up and with horror I see he's trying to record the fight.

'That's my boyfriend!' I scream and try to twist out of Adam's grip but he holds on like a vice. I turn back to the fight in time to see Jason rush Joe, but he's ready for him this time and turns his head so that it just glances off his jaw then lands a punch straight on Jason's nose, then stands back as the other boy staggers, nearly on his knees. Now he's bleeding, and I feel sick. This is horrible.

Joe however is stepping away, apparently satisfied he's got the better of him. I sigh with relief, sagging against Adam who still hasn't let go. At least he's not trying to cop a feel.

'Get off her. Now,' Joe says, stepping towards us. Then Jason speaks, his voice dripping with scorn.

'Yeah, go on, go running to your little slag. Leave some for me, yeah?'

I close my eyes in distress at his words and the look of sheer rage that crosses Joe's face when he hears them. When I open them again I see everything as if in slow motion.

Joe strides over to Jason, who looks panicked as if he wasn't expecting him to come back and swings at Joe wildly. The punch connects with the side of his head but Joe barely seems to notice it and doesn't break his stride. He grabs Jason's collar and raises his fist, ready to smash it directly into his face. Jason looks terrified. But it's Joe's face that scares me. His eyes are wild, his pupils so dilated they look black and his mouth is set in a grim line. I don't recognise him. I open my mouth to shout but nothing comes out.

Time stands still, and all I'm aware of is my heartbeat thundering in my ears and Joe's fist poised to smash into Jason's face. At that distance, with the power in Joe's strong body, he'll break his nose or worse.

If he gets into any more trouble he'll hate himself. Finally, I find my voice.

'Joe, don't!' I scream.

Something flickers in his eyes and he looks over at me, then back at Jason, who's cowering now. Slowly he lowers his fist and I let out a breath I didn't know I'd been holding. He pushes the other boy away.

'You're not worth it,' he snarls, and spits at the ground near his feet, then turns to me. I smile at him and see the relief in his eyes, the anger draining out of them. I step towards him with my hand outstretched and Adam lets me go.

Just as Jason rushes at him from behind. I scream a warning, but he doesn't need it. Joe spins and tackles him to the ground in one fluid movement.

Behind me, someone claps.

Jason drags himself to his feet, bloody and bruised and looking ashamed. Next to me Adam is shaking his head.

'Coward,' he says, and turns around and walks off. As Joe comes over to me the crowd begins to disperse. To my surprise Jason goes over to Joe with his hand out. I watch in bemusement as they slap hands and then each other's backs, nodding at each other. Boy code again. Jason slinks off with a few of his friends and Joe walks over to me. He looks tired and his clothes are torn and his lip bleeding but I have never seen him look so gorgeous. I go straight into his arms, burying my head in his chest, my heart bubbling up with pride. Not because he won the fight, but because he stopped before he went too far. How could I ever have doubted him? My eyes are wet as he lifts my face to look at him.

'I'm sorry,' he whispers. 'I should have told you about Dannii. I didn't want to cause trouble.'

I kiss him carefully, trying not to hurt his cut lip but savouring the warmth of his mouth on mine.

'I should have trusted you.' I say, and his eyes cloud over. He looks so hurt I feel like I've kicked a puppy.

'I can't believe you thought I would do something like that. I love you, Ash, you're my girl.'

His words make me cry again. He kisses the tears from my eyes and then claims my mouth again and we fall on each other like we're starving for touch, his cut mouth forgotten. His hands make fists in my hair and I moan into his mouth. Already he's hard against me and I pull away laughing.

'Down boy!' I giggle, glad that for girls our arousal isn't so blatant. Joe doesn't look one bit abashed though, pulling me back to him and cupping the swell of my butt with his hands.

'I'm crazy about you, Ash,' he says seriously. 'Promise me that you won't run off like that again. If there's a problem, talk to me.'

'I will,' I promise.

We're pretty much alone now, all the spectators having

wandered off leaving just a few younger teenagers smoking by the swings. I reach up and touch his lip where it's cut and swollen. It's not as bad as it first looked.

'You need to put something on it.'

'I'll wash it, it'll be fine. Come back here.' His hands trail over my butt, kneading and squeezing, his fingers brushing the inside of my thighs. He pulls me into him, and he's still hard.

'Come back home with me,' he whispers, and in answer I take his hand and we start walking. We say very little on the way to his. There isn't much to say.

We go up to his room still hand in hand, still in silence, and then he turns to me and takes off his torn shirt. I touch his lip again.

'You should wash it.'

'After,' he says and reaches for me. He kisses my neck lightly and starts to tug my top out of my jeans. I help him, raising my arms so he can take it off and then unclipping my bra myself and tossing it to one side. He lifts my breasts carefully in his hands and rubs his thumbs over my nipples until they're hard and tingling, then he pushes them together, lowers his head and flicks his tongue across both of them in turn.

'That feels really good,' I whisper, a total understatement. His mouth and hands turn my body into a hot core of need and I fumble at his zip, wrapping my hand around his erection as it springs free and being rewarded with a gasp of 'God, Ash'. I run my thumb over the head of him, amazed at how it can be so hard yet the skin silky soft. I walk backwards towards the bed and he comes with me, pushing my bottoms down over my hips. As we reach the edge of the bed he kneels in front of me and pulls them down and off my feet, then he kisses a trail of butterflies up my thigh and across the hem of my knickers, slipping his hand inside them as he stands up.

'Condom?' I ask. He groans and leans away to pull a fresh packet from his drawer. He must have bought them yesterday, knowing I was coming round. He rips one open and I reach for it.

'Can I try?' I ask and he hands it to me. It takes a couple of attempts but I get it on and sit back for a minute, admiring my handiwork. Joe laughs and pushes me back onto the bed.

It doesn't hurt at all this time. I'm ready for him and he feels thick and snug inside me. He's careful though, moving slowly and looking into my eyes the whole time.

'I love you,' he strokes my face and I turn my head and nip at his thumb.

'Love you too,' I say, and then he picks up his pace and I can't talk at all.

Afterwards we get dressed, smiling at each other the whole time. I watch him as if I could drink him in with my eyes.

'What shall we do tonight?' he asks, and I grin, thinking that I know exactly what we can do. Then I have another idea.

'Come to mine,' I say, 'for dinner.'

He looks surprised.

'Really? Won't your mum hate me after all this?'

I shake my head, thinking she's more likely to say, 'I told you so'.

'Okay,' he says, and his face splits into a dazzling smile. God, I love him.

Mum looks up as we walk in, looking surprised as she sees Joe but quickly plastering a smile onto her face.

'Pleased to meet you Mrs Evans.'

He holds his hand out politely, giving her his most charming smile, and I see her melt.

It's not all going to be easy, I know that. I still have to deal with Dannii, and get used to Matt, and work through my exhilarating yet terrifying feelings for Joe. But I also know I won't be doing it alone.

We're in this together, all the way.

LODESTONE
BOOKS

Lodestone Books is a new imprint, which offers a broad spectrum of subjects in YA/NA literature. Compelling reading, the Teen/Young/New Adult reader is sure to find something edgy, enticing and innovative. From dystopian societies, through a whole range of fantasy, horror, science fiction and paranormal fiction, all the way to the other end of the sphere, historical drama, steam-punk adventure, and everything in between. You'll find stories of crime, coming of age and contemporary romance. Whatever your preference you will discover it here.